T0015565

TREASURY
OF FOLKLORE
STARS
& SKIES

For Sally

First published in the United Kingdom in 2023 by
B.T. Batsford
43 Great Ormond Street
London WC1N 3HZ

An imprint of B.T. Batsford Holdings Ltd

Illustrations by Joe McLaren

ISBN 9781849947749

A CIP catalogue record for this book is available from the British Library.

10 9 8 7 6 5 4 3 2 1

Reproduction by Rival Colour, UK
Printed by Vivar Printing Sdn, Bhd., Malaysia

This book can be ordered direct from the publisher at
www.batsford.com, or try your local bookshop

TREASURY
OF FOLKLORE
STARS
& SKIES

WILLOW WINSHAM

BATSFORD

CONTENTS

INTRODUCTION:
A Journey Through the Skies

Who has not paused for at least one moment in their lives to gaze upwards in awe at the great vastness of the skies above? Whether it is to marvel at a rainbow, seek out the familiar pattern of a well-known constellation or to check whether rain is on the way, for that brief pause in our busy lives, we are at one with the cosmos, linked to every other being that has done the same since time began. During the day, the sun shines its life-giving light down upon us, while at night we are treated to the shimmering spectacle of the stars and the light of the moon. And as we look upwards in awe and perhaps a little fear, we find ourselves unwittingly linked with every other person who is doing or has ever done likewise – whether in our own times or many thousands of years ago.

For the resplendent canopy of the skies and heavens has been of monumental importance to humankind since time immemorial. First, the stars: guiding people as they travel on their way, pinpointing their location in the vastness of the sea or desert in the earliest of navigational systems. Then there is the weather: the power of the elements determining whether we have access to food and water supplies and, in the extreme of storms and blizzards, threatening our very existence. Our gods and goddesses have likewise resided in the skies in their heavenly splendour: the complex beauty of the cosmos cannot, we think, have been by accident. The constellations must have been placed and designed; there can be no other explanation in our minds, for how could something so intricate have happened by coincidence?

Tales and stories, legends and myths, sayings and superstitions have poured forth from hundreds of different cultures, belief systems and ideas, blending into a melting pot of folklore not unlike the swirling symphony of the universe itself. It is through these tales and ideas that we try to answer the all-consuming questions such as: where does the sun come from? How did the Milky Way come to be? Who are we, and what is our place is this vast, great universe? Too great to comprehend, we could spend a lifetime trying to make sense of it all and still only grasp a fragment of what is out there: through these stories and ideas we have woven ourselves a rich legacy that perfectly bears testament to the splendour of the skies.

Throughout these pages then, leave the safety of solid ground behind, and take a journey upwards to soar through the wonders that are above us. From frightening creatures and battling gods to shooting stars, constellations and brilliantly dancing lights, prepare to enter the great unknown. And as we explore this celestial realm, listen for the whispers of our ancestors, the sayings and superstitions we still follow today, the origin stories; perhaps long-forgotten, but remembered each time we follow and share them, part of us and our shared cultural heritage forever.

It would be impossible to cover every piece of folklore related to the stars and skies in one volume, and to attempt to do so would be to do a great injustice to both source material and readers alike. Regrettably, therefore, many fascinating pieces of information and stories have not made it to these pages; what you will find, however, is a carefully selected, painstakingly researched and lovingly presented selection of tales and beliefs that illuminate once again how folklore is truly the tie that binds us together across time and space.

PART ONE
THE STARS AND HEAVENS

THE SUN, MOON
AND STARS

According to the Navajo (or Diné, meaning 'The People') in the Fifth World, the First People had four lights. The yellow light came from the western mountains, white light rose over the eastern mountains, blue light came from the southern mountains, while darkness spread from the north. These lights had been brought from the lower world and gave out no heat, which meant the temperature was the same during both day and night.

The people were unhappy with this situation and complained that they needed more light. In answer to their complaints, First Woman found a solution. She sent out four creatures, Glow-worm to the east, Fox Fire to the south, Lightning Beetle to the west and Firefly to the north, to give extra light to anyone who might need it.

This solution proved only temporary, however, and soon the people were complaining once more. The lights, they said, were too small or too flickering or too dim, and they were not happy. First Woman again thought of how she could please them, and finally sent a messenger to Fire Man. Fire Man lit up the land around Fire Mountain, but the people were not happy with the smoke and the heat that it gave off, and again were unsatisfied with First Woman's solution.

Realizing that she would have to find another way to light the earth, First Woman consulted with wise men to make a plan. She sent out helpers to bring back a great flat slab of rock, with the stipulation that it must be the largest, hardest, most unbreakable rock to be had. Her helpers travelled far and wide, before finally returning, bringing with them an enormous flat slab of quartz.

It was big enough for her purpose, and First Woman marked out two round wheels of equal size. Then came the task of cutting them out. It was difficult; the quartz was hard and the work was slow with their stone hammers and sharp flints, but finally it was done, and two flat discs lay ready on the ground.

First Man and First Woman then decorated each of the stones according to the powers that they would be given. The first disc was marked with blue turquoise to make heat, and red coral tied to it and set around the rim. Then a horn was placed on each side, one to hold male rain and the other male lightning. Feathers were tied to its rim so it could be carried through the sky and spread heat and light to east, west, north and south. At the top and bottom were four zigzag lines of male wind and rain, and finally four sunspots placed for guardians.

First Man declared it finished, and blessed it with mixed pollens and a song by the lark, to be known thereafter as the 'sun's voice'. This was all very well, pointed out First Woman, but it had still to be set in place in the sky. There was some debate over how this could be done, as no one seemed to know, but Fire Man then suggested carrying the disc to the top of the highest mountain to be placed there. From the highest peak it could shine on the whole of the earth at once. Once this was agreed, the disc was taken to the eastern mountains, and there it was attached to the sky securely with lightning darts.

Now the second disc needed to be decorated. First Woman said that, unlike the first, it would be cool and moist, as they did not need another bearing heat and light. This disc was therefore decorated differently: covered with white shell, yellow pollen in a band on its chin, and the rim decorated with red coral. Feathers were attached to take the disc's weight, and horns attached containing female lightning and winds. At the top and bottom were placed four straight lines, giving the disc control over the summer rains. The second disc was likewise taken to the top of a mountain in the east and secured to the sky with lightning.

Although First Woman had been certain now that the people would be satisfied at last, unfortunately this was not to be, and the complaints continued. It was unfair, they said, that the sun was to stay in the same place all of the time, as this meant that one side of the land would always be summer, while the other would always be winter. It became clear from this that the two discs needed to move across the sky, but the problem was obvious: how could this be done when they were made of stone and lacked a spirit?

As all were contemplating the problem, two men, very old and very wise, came forward. They offered their own spirits to the sun and the moon, giving them the power to move across the sky as the people wanted. The spirit of one of the men entered the sun disc and was known as Jóhonaa'éí, Sun Bearer, while the other entered the moon disc and was called Tł'éé'honaa'éí, Moon Bearer. The stone discs began to shake and tremble, but there was still more to decide before they could do what they were meant to.

Both the sun and moon wanted to know how they would know where to go, which path they should take through the skies. First Man came up with the solution: each was given twelve feathers from the eagle's tail, so they would guide them as they guided the eagle. Sun started on his journey first, while moon waited all day until sun had reached the western mountains. As moon was finally about to start on his own journey, Wind Boy decided to give a helping hand. Standing behind moon, he blew a stiff breeze; instead of helping, however, it blew the feathers across moon's face, obscuring his view. Moon could only follow the tips of the feathers, now pointing in all different directions; and he has followed uneven paths across the sky ever since.

And so the sun and the moon took their places in the sky and made their first journeys across the heavens.

Where the two discs had been cut, there remained myriad small chips of stone, dust and debris, covering the blanket beneath them. First Woman declared that these should not be wasted: they would be used to make more lights in the sky.

They set to work once more, and the stars were shaped one by one. First Woman decided that she would use them to write the laws that would rule humankind for all eternity, as they would not be erased with time and would be visible and remembered for evermore.

Once First Woman had traced in the sand the path each star was to take, and First Man had tied a prayer feather on the upper point of each star, they were ready to be set in the sky. Some were placed alone, others in constellations, and Fire Man climbed up and down the ladder, setting each in its allotted place in the sky above.

The whole process took a great deal of time. Coyote, growing impatient, complained to First Woman that things were taking far too long. If he helped, he insisted, it would be finished much quicker. First Woman was not keen on this idea, reminding Coyote that he was prone to mistakes and that trouble often followed. Coyote promised that he would follow her exact instructions, however, and First Woman finally agreed.

Unfortunately, things did not quite go to plan. First Woman gave Coyote two identical stars, the twins, set to run on paths alongside each other. While climbing the ladder, Coyote grew dizzy and almost fell. Then Wind Boy shook the ladder, which made Coyote place both stars in one hand in order to carry on climbing. When he reached the top, alas, he could not tell which star was which, or which to place where. So Coyote placed them at random, but it was immediately clear that they were in the wrong places: a loud, terrible grating noise began as the stars tried their hardest to switch places with each other. Unable to reach them, Coyote returned down the ladder, the stars crossing in front of each other so they could run on the paths they were meant to.

First Woman was greatly displeased, and scolded Coyote and sent him away. She then continued to make more star patterns, representing nearly all the animals, birds and insects on earth. Each was given a spark of fire by the burning coals of Fire Man's torch, so they would always be able to find their way.

Finally First Woman gave Fire Man many stone fragments, and he took them up the ladder. They were too small and there were far too many of them for him to place one by one. Instead, Fire Man gave to each a spark of fire before throwing them in handfuls against the sky.

Then Coyote intervened once more. He grasped the blanket by two corners and swung it high; the remaining fragments and dust arced across the sky, forming the Milky Way or Yikáísdáhá – 'That Which Awaits the Dawn', a pathway for spirits to travel between heaven and earth.

First Woman then decreed that one man from every generation should learn the laws in order to interpret them and tell others what they meant. This important knowledge would then be passed down to a younger man who would then in turn pass the laws down to another and so on and so on, in order that they would never be forgotten.

SOLAR DEITIES:
Gods and Goddesses of the Sun

The largest object in our solar system, the sun is the source of all life on earth, looked upon with awe and fear by humankind throughout the ages. Common across many of the world's cultures is the belief in a sun god or goddess, in many cases a personification of the fiery giant around which we orbit. From Japan's Amaterasu to the Lithuanian Saule, here are a few of the most fascinating solar deities from world mythology.

Amaterasu

'Great Divinity Illuminating Heaven', Amaterasu or, to give the goddess her full name, Amaterasu-Omikami, is one of the most important deities in the Japanese Shinto pantheon. Goddess of the rising sun, she is inextricably linked with the Shinto state and imperial family.

Amaterasu was born of Izanagi, the Japanese creator kami or god. When his wife, Izanami, died giving birth to the fire god Kagutsuchi, the grieving Izanagi journeyed to the underworld, Yomotsukuni, to try to bring her back; he was ultimately unsuccessful, however, and returned alone to the upper world. As Izanagi cleansed himself from the taint of death he washed his left eye, and thus Amaterasu was born. Amaterasu's two siblings came forth in a similar fashion: Tsukiyomi when Izanagi washed his right eye, and Susanoo when he washed his nose. Susanoo, the storm god, was given control of the sea, and Tsukiyomi was the god of the moon.

Susanoo, mischievous and provocative by nature, proved to be a perpetual thorn in his sister Amaterasu's side. On one occasion, Susanoo visited Amaterasu in heaven. Amaterasu was understandably wary, thinking her brother came to challenge her position, and met him with a display of military might. Susanoo, however, insisted he came in peace, suggesting instead that they procreate together in order to cement good feeling on each side. Agreeing to the plan, Amaterasu broke Susanoo's sword into three pieces and swallowed them, before breathing out a mist from which three females were born. Susanoo, for his part, chewed the jewels that belonged to his sister, and breathed out five male children, which Amaterasu claimed as her own.

Although this was meant to increase goodwill towards each other, Susanoo soon revealed his true colours. He carried out a series of increasingly intolerable acts against his sister: breaking down the divisions in Amaterasu's rice fields, defecating on her chair, and finally, the last straw, removing the roof of her weaving room and tossing a flayed horse inside, which led to the death of one of her attendants. This was too much for the goddess. Angry Amaterasu shut herself in a cave and refused to come out, plunging the world into terrible darkness. There she stayed, steadfastly ignoring the entreaties of the other gods. Everyone despaired, and began to think of ways to entice the goddess out into the world again.

The first attempt was to place several cocks outside the cave in the hope that when they crowed the goddess would think it was dawn and time for her to rise. When this failed, the gods tried again; this time they placed a large sakaki tree hung with bright jewels, white clothes and a mirror close to the entrance of the cave, hoping to lure her out with the magnificence of her own reflection. The goddess Ame-no-Uzume, in a trance, danced riotously and started to disrobe, making the other gods laugh and creating a great ruckus. The noise at last piqued Amaterasu's interest and she

opened the cave: as the other gods had hoped, she caught sight of herself in the mirror and was transfixed. Another god seized his chance and pulled Amaterasu out into the open, returning light to the world once more. To prevent her from returning to the cave, the gods threw down a sacred rope made of rice straw – *shimenawa* – in front of the entrance.

Amaterasu is also closely linked with the introduction of rice to Japan. It is said that she sent Tsukiyomi, originally meant to rule the heavens with her, down to earth to watch Ukemochi, a food goddess, to see what she was doing. Unfortunately, when the goddess offered him rice, fish and game that she had vomited from her own mouth, Tsukiyomi grew offended and slew Ukemochi. Furious, Amaterasu refused to see her brother again, and the sun and the moon were never seen at the same time from that day. There was some benefit to come from Ukemochi's death, however: when the body of the slain goddess was inspected, it was discovered that various things had sprung forth from it, including silkworms from her eyebrows, the horse and cow from her head, rice from her stomach, and beans and wheat from her genitals. These were brought back to heaven to Amaterasu, who took the rice and created the first holy rice fields in Heaven.

The emperors of Japan to this day claim descent from Amaterasu. The first Emperor of Japan, Jimmu, was said to have descended from Ninigi, Amaterasu's grandson. This celestial connection is reflected in the name of the emperors, Amatsuhitsugi, meaning 'heavenly sun heir'. The Imperial regalia – the Yata no Kagami, the mirror that was used to lure Amaterasu from the cave; the Yasakani no Magatama, her jewels; and Kusanagi no Tsurugi, Susanoo's sword – were also said to have been gifted from Amaterasu to Ninigi, and then passed to the first emperor. The nobility also claim descent from the goddess, via the deities that she and her brother Susanoo produced together.

As further evidence of her status, Amaterasu is worshipped at the most important Shinto shrine in Japan, the Ise Grand Shrine. Millions of visitors and pilgrims visit the shrine each year.

Saule

According to Latvian and Lithuanian tradition, Saule was the sun goddess and also the goddess of life and fertility. She married Menes, god of the moon, but unfortunately he didn't remain faithful to her for long and, according to Lithuanian tradition, had an affair with Aušrinė, the goddess of the dawn. According to one version of the story, Perkūnas, the thunder god, avenged the slighted goddess, tearing the unfaithful moon god to pieces in punishment.

In Lithuania, Saule is mentioned in *The Chronicle* by John Malalas, one of the earliest written sources for Lithuanian mythology. Saule also appears frequently in the *dainas*, Latvian folk songs numbering around 300,000 in total, and which provide much of what is known about folk beliefs in Latvia: at least 1,500 mention her directly. An even greater number of the *dainas* refer to the sun itself, both highlighting the importance of the celestial body and the goddess associated with it, in a mythological and cultural context. It is from these songs that the majority of the information about Saule comes, although there is some debate regarding the balance between what is true inherited folk belief and later invention.

Saule is frequently associated with the colour red: overnight, she is said to don a garment of this colour, and thus rises red in the morning. She was also said to be wreathed in a garland of red flowers during the feast of Ligo, the major festival celebrating the summer solstice and honouring the goddess on 23 June. In many depictions, Saule wears national dress, in silver or gold silk, with a crown on her head, which she hangs on a tree in the evening. Saule is generally portrayed as a benevolent mother goddess, known for showing compassion and pity towards humankind.

In her solar role, Saule makes her daily journey through the forests on a chariot, drawn by inexhaustible horses of varying number: two or three yellow horses, two, five or six brown horses, two grey or even a single small horse are mentioned depending on the source. As evening comes, and the day draws to a close, Saule pauses to let her horses wash in the sea, and she sits atop a hill with their golden reins held in her hands as they do so. As night falls, she changes her mode of transportation and travels across waters such as lakes, rivers and the sea, riding a golden boat.

Saule was known to cry frequently, these episodes attributed to a number of reasons, such as the departure of her daughter for her marriage, leaves blowing from a birch tree, a golden apple falling to the ground or her boat sinking in the sea. The Žaltys snake was known to be associated with Saule; it was bad luck to kill one, and good luck to have one in your house.

According to one legend, the smith named Teliavelis created the sun in his forge, before throwing it up into the sky.

Utu-Shamash

This Sumerian solar deity was known by the Mesopotamians as Utu, and later by the Akkadian name Shamash or Šamaš, and was one of the most important gods in the Mesopotamian pantheon. Mention of Utu can be found as early as around 3,500 BCE in the first Sumerian writings in existence, and he is referenced in a variety of sources, from royal hymns to documentation of business transactions. So important was he that in the law codes of the Babylonian ruler Hammurabi it is stated that the god was responsible for giving the laws to humankind.

In Sumerian tradition, Utu was the son of the moon god, Nanna, while Akkadian belief names his father as Anu or Enlil. Utu had a twin sister, Inanna, the goddess of war and love. Some sources also attribute further siblings to the god: a brother, Ishkur the god of storms; and Ereshkigal, the Queen of the Dead, is also sometimes said to be a sibling of Utu. His wife is Serida, or Aya in Akkadian, the dawn goddess. Several children were attributed to the god, including Kittum, the personification of truth, and Sisig, the god of dreams.

Utu is most commonly depicted as an old, bearded, long-armed man, with rays of light shining from his shoulders. He was also sometimes shown as a disc with wings, or the sun itself. The solar disc is portrayed as a circle, with four points in each of the four directions and four waved lines protruding diagonally between each of these points, representing the might and power of the sun. On some cylinder seals, Utu is seen holding a large pruning saw, an arc-shaped blade with large, jagged teeth; another of his emblems.

In earlier references, the god was said to make his journey across the heavens on foot. As time went on, however, this changed to the belief that he rode through the skies in a chariot of fire each day. As each morning came around anew, the huge gates of heaven resting on a mountain opened in the east, flung wide by two gods. Shamash took his place in his chariot and rode it across the sky as the day progressed, moving steadily towards the west, marking the path of the sun. Arriving there at the end of the day, the gates in the west were duly opened for him, and he went inside to rest.

Utu's chariot was pulled by four fiery beasts – generally held to be horses or mules, though one argument has been made for them being lions. These beasts were named Uhegalanna, 'the abundant light of heaven'; Uhushgalanna, 'the terrifying great light of heaven'; Usurmurgalanna, 'the dreadful great light of heaven'; and Unirgalanna, 'the noble light of heaven'. The god driving his chariot was named Bunene, and in some accounts he is also Utu's son.

Utu-Shamash was known as the god of justice, and in that role was said to be a just and wise judge. It was a natural role for him to take; just like the strong heat of the sun penetrating everywhere and everything, so the sun god knew and saw everything that went on upon the earth, thus putting him in the unique position to judge humankind and gods alike.

Utu also featured strongly in many sacrificial divination rituals, and the god was frequently asked to help provide an answer to a variety of questions. Around 350 queries survive from the Neo-Assyrian period (9th–7th century BCE) when kings Esarhaddon and Ashurbanipal consulted him frequently, with concerns about illnesses, rebellions and the loyalty of those beneath them. Utu's aid was also called for to help protect against curses and evil wishes.

In one Sumerian poem, Utu is portrayed in a light somewhat different from usual; he attempts – and ultimately fails – to seduce his twin sister Inanna by getting her drunk.

Huītzilōpōchtli

Huītzilōpōchtli was the sun god of the Mexica people, better known by their later name of the Aztecs. He was also the god of war and human sacrifice, and, through his choice of weapon, Xiuhcoatl, the fire serpent, was associated with fire. Huītzilōpōchtli was very much an Aztec-specific god; mention of him is not found outside of the valley of Mexico, and depictions of the god are noticeably absent from the art and artefacts of the rest of ancient Mesoamerica.

There is some debate regarding the exact meaning of his name, but it is generally translated as 'left-handed hummingbird' or sometimes 'Hummingbird of the south', from *huitzilin* – 'hummingbird', and *opočhtli*, 'left-hand side'. Some suggest that a more accurate translation is 'the left or south side of the hummingbird'. The god was also known as Xiuhpilli – 'Turquoise Prince'.

In appearance, Huītzilōpōchtli was generally depicted with a hummingbird headdress of blue-green, a golden tiara and white heron feathers. He had blue and white striped paint on his face and a black mask around his eyes, dotted with stars. He was also often depicted holding his fire serpent.

Perhaps the best-known tale about Huītzilōpōchtli is the story of his birth. There are various differences across versions, but essentially the details are thus. One day his mother, Cōātlīcue – meaning 'she of the serpent skirt', due to the skirt she wore made of woven snakes – was sweeping at Coatepec, Snake Mountain. To her surprise, a ball of hummingbird feathers descended towards her. Cōātlīcue caught them in her hand and, entranced by their beauty, placed them in her waistband for safekeeping. When she went to remove them later, however, the feathers had vanished. She had been impregnated by the feathers, and was now with child. When her existing children – the Centzon Huitznahua, the 400 stars of the south, and daughter Coyolxāuhqui – discovered their mother's condition, they were outraged, angered greatly that she had dishonoured herself and them, especially when she refused to name the father of her child. Their mother had brought such shame upon them, said Coyolxāuhqui, that the only thing they could do to rectify the situation was to kill her. Learning of their plan, Cōātlīcue was understandably terrified, but help was at hand. Her unborn child, Huītzilōpōchtli, communicated with her from the womb, assuring her that he was ready to fight to protect her and himself against his treacherous half-siblings.

Thus Cōātlīcue waited atop the mountain for her children to attack. She did not have to wait long, and they came charging up towards her. At the very moment they reached the top, Cōātlīcue gave birth to Huītzilōpōchtli – in some versions her head was struck from her body and the god sprang forth. The god, however, was no mere babe; he came forth fully formed and armed ready to fight for his mother, just as he had promised. Wielding his great weapon, the fire serpent, Huītzilōpōchtli killed his sister and cut off her head, her slain body falling down the mountain to the bottom. He then chased off his brothers, killing huge numbers of them as they tried to escape.

According to Aztec mythology, Huītzilōpōchtli was also responsible for what would become known as the Aztec people establishing their home. He instructed the people of Aztlan to set off on a pilgrimage that would turn out to last for generations, taking them through many hardships, battles and divisions along the way. Their end point was clear, however: they were to establish a new capital in a very specific place. They would know it by seeing an eagle sitting on a cactus eating a snake. Their wanderings finally came to an end in 1345, when Tenochtitlan – 'the place where the gods were created' – was founded.

Controversially, the Aztecs believed that regular human sacrifices had to be made to Huītzilōpōchtli in order to keep the eternal night at bay. According to Aztec belief this was necessary as the god was constantly chasing the stars and moon; if he did not have the strength to fight his siblings, they would be triumphant, and the world would be destroyed.

In 1978, the ruins of the Aztec capital, Tenochtitlan, were discovered beneath Mexico City. The Great Temple, Templo Mayor, was the greatest find, dedicated to Huītzilōpōchtli and Tlaloc, the rain god. Among the finds there was a huge, sculpted stone disc 3.25m (over 10ft) across, showing the events of the sun god's birth and the battle that followed, including a depiction of the dismembered body of his sister at bottom of the staircase that leads up to the Huītzilōpōchtli shrine.

Sól

Sól was the Germanic goddess of the sun, featuring heavily in Norse mythology relating to Ragnarok, the end of the world. Sól was fated to be chased through the sky by the wolf Sköll and, according to myth, a solar eclipse is caused when the wolf draws close enough to snap at her. Sól's brother Máni, the moon, is likewise chased by Hati, the wolves snapping at their horse-drawn chariots until they are finally caught, ushering in the end of the world. All is not lost, however, as it is foretold that before the end comes, Sól will give birth to a daughter – even more brilliant in beauty and brightness than herself – who will shine on in her mother's stead in the new world.

Sól and Máni were originally children of Mundilfari, named after the sun and moon due to their exquisite beauty. But alas, the gods were deeply offended by such a display of arrogance and intervened, decreeing that Sól and her brother should be placed in the heavens themselves. They were charged with driving the two horses that drew the sun's chariot – Arvakr and Alsvior, crossing the heavens each day to mark the passing of the days and years for humankind.

Sól was referred to by several names, including day-star disc, fair-wheel, elf-disc and ever-glow, and is referenced in both the *Prose Edda* and *Poetic Edda*. Although Sól is referred to as a goddess in several instances, and the sun was generally venerated, it is not believed that there was a Germanic sun cult as witnessed in other areas.

A FATEFUL FLIGHT:
Daedalus and Icarus

According to Greek mythology, Daedalus – his name aptly meaning 'skilfully wrought' – was an architect, sculptor and inventor. Banished from Athens for the murder of his nephew and apprentice, Daedalus found himself in Crete with his son, Icarus. There he was caught up in the great drama attached to King Minos and his family. For Minos had angered the sea god, Poseidon: the god had given the king a white bull to sacrifice, but Minos had kept it for himself. As punishment, the angered god got his own back by making the king's wife attracted to the bull; calling on Daedalus's skill, the queen entreated him to make a wooden cow in which she could conceal herself and thus mate with the white bull. Her plan was successful, and the queen found herself pregnant: in time, she bore the monstrous Minotaur, half-human, but with the terrible head of a bull. Daedalus's talents were again called upon, this time by the king, who ordered the building of the legendary Labyrinth in which to keep the monster far away from sight.

All was well until the hero Theseus arrived – he was intended as a sacrifice to the terrible beast, but things did not go according to plan, as Minos's daughter, Ariadne, fell in love with him. She in turn called upon Daedalus, begging him to reveal the secrets of the Labyrinth so that Theseus could escape with his life. Daedalus helped her and the plan was successful: Theseus escaped, taking Ariadne with him. King Minos was so angered by this that he shut Daedalus and Icarus up in the Labyrinth. The queen released them, but they were stranded, unable to leave Crete by sea or by land as both were under the control of Minos.

Greatly troubled by their exiled condition, Daedalus hit upon a plan. For there was one sphere that the wily Minos did not command: the air. And so Daedalus set to work. He gathered feathers and arranged them in rows: small and short first, increasing gradually in length and size in the manner of a set of reed pipes or, indeed, wings. Thread and wax were used to hold these wondrous creations together: the whole curved into shape in imitation of the birds whose freedom he envied so greatly.

As Daedalus worked, his son Icarus watched on with fascination, often toying with his father's materials and hindering his progress. At last, though, the wings were complete, and the time of their escape into the sky and freedom drew near. The fearful father gave his son many instructions, the most important being to maintain a course not too high and not too low, for fear that the waves or the sun would bring him to an untimely end. He, Daedalus, would lead the way; all Icarus need do was follow his father and they would be safe and free. Unable to prepare his son any further, there was no more time for delay. Daedalus attached the wings to his son and then himself, before launching himself into the sky.

Those who they passed looked up in wonder, marvelling at what they saw and thinking the pair to be gods as they flew past. Father and son made good progress, and it seemed as if they would make their escape as planned. However, it was not to be. For Icarus, with all the fearlessness and arrogance of youth, found the power of flight too exhilarating: forgetting to be careful, he flew from his father's steady path, straying higher and higher. Alas, he could not continue so: the wax, so carefully applied, melted in the heat of the sun, and the feathers lost their formation, falling away. With nothing now to keep him airborne, the ill-fated young man fell, crying out for his father, into the unforgiving waters below.

Unaware of his son's terrible fate, Daedalus called and called for him, until he spotted the heartbreaking sight of the feathers in the water. How Daedalus wept for his son! Blaming himself most harshly, he retrieved and buried Icarus's body in a place nearby, and the land was afterwards known as Icaria, in remembrance of the one who rested there and all that had been lost.

SUN-GOT-BIT-BY-BEAR:
Eclipses of the Sun

The sun, ever present, has been one of the daily constants for humankind for the entirety of our history. Only, sometimes, this brightly burning star does the unthinkable: it seems to wane, diminishing before our very eyes and even vanishing altogether, plunging the world into darkness with no promise that it will return again. For thousands of years people all over the world have held their breath upon a solar eclipse, creating countless tales and explanations for this fearful phenomenon. Even today, when science provides an answer for the causes of a solar eclipse – when the moon is directly between the earth and the sun and the moon casts a shadow over the earth – we still pause, waiting for the moment that the sun shines bright upon us once more.

In written sources, some of the oldest mentions of a solar eclipse come from Ancient China over 4,000 years ago, where it was believed that an eclipse was caused by a dragon eating the sun: one such early description states that 'the sun has been eaten'. In a common approach to eclipses, people would bang drums loudly and make lots of noise in an attempt to scare the dragon away and bring back the sun.

The idea of the sun being eaten is a very common theme in eclipse folklore across the globe. In Armenia it was also believed that an eclipse was caused by a dragon chasing and eating the sun. A Berber story from northern Africa tells of a huge, winged, evil jinni that lurks in an underground lair. From there it soars skywards, swallowing the sun whole. In a definite case of being careful what you eat, it cannot stomach this hot meal and vomits forth its prize, leaving the sun free to shine again.

In a Chahta tale from North America, a black squirrel is said to be to blame, causing an eclipse of the sun as it nibbles and gnaws at it. The word used for eclipse by the Pomo, the indigenous people of northern California, translates as 'Sun-got-bit-by-bear'. In this tale, a bear and the sun have a falling out; the bear bumps into the sun, and when the sun tells the bear to stand aside, the bear refuses, telling the sun in turn that it should be the one to move. As stubborn as each other, neither will shift, and the two fall to fighting. In the ensuing ruckus the bear grabs the sun and, chewing on it, causes an eclipse.

According to Hindu mythology, eclipses are caused by the demon Rahu. Rahu stole an immortality elixir, *amrita*, so he could live forever. He was caught in the act of drinking it, and had only partially swallowed it before Vishnu beheaded him with his flying disc. Rahu's body perished, but his severed head was immortal, never to die or find rest. To this day he floats around the cosmos, causing an eclipse when he consumes the sun. Pots and pans are banged to make him cough up the sun and go away again.

In a Buryat version from Siberia, Rahu, known as Alkha, spent his time chasing after the sun and moon, periodically swallowing them and causing an eclipse. Irritated by this behaviour, the gods finally chopped him in two. Although his lower body dropped down to earth, his head lives on, still munching on the sun and moon, causing their eclipses, although they don't last for long as Alkha has no body to hold them in. Similarly in Polynesia and Indonesia, Kala Rau eats the sun: thankfully he burns his tongue and spits it back out again, the world saved from darkness until next time.

In Korean mythology, both solar and lunar eclipses are caused by *bulgae* or fierce fire dogs. A pack of these creatures was ordered by the king of the heavenly kingdom of Gamangnara – Dark World – to steal the sun so that it could not affect the darkness surrounding his own kingdom. They were not successful in capturing it, but the king did not give up and sent a new dog each time: when the dogs managed to bite the sun, an eclipse was the result.

In South America, the Chiqutoan Manasi people of eastern Bolivia believed celestial serpents attacking the sun caused an eclipse. If they were successful, ultimate darkness would follow: then humankind would be turned into hair-covered animals and eventually be wiped out.

Solar eclipses weren't always caused by the sun being eaten or bitten. According to some indigenous groups of the Pampas in central Argentina, an eclipse of the sun was caused by a great bird spreading its massive wings over it. For the Fon people of Benin, western Africa, the male sun and female moon love each other deeply, but due to their busy lives, they very rarely get to meet. When they do, they make the most of their time together, but turn off the light so they can be together in privacy. Some believe that an eclipse occurs when the sun itself cannot bear to witness the terrible tragedies of history, and temporarily turns its face away: it is said that the sun was eclipsed during the Crucifixion and when Adam and Eve were expelled from the Garden of Eden. A belief from Armenia held that a sorcerer could enchant the sun – and moon – to stop their light, halting them in their tracks or even bringing them down from the sky altogether.

Understandably, eclipses were generally looked upon as a bad omen, often seen as a sign of great disaster to come. In Ancient Mesopotamia, there was a practice of having substitute kings prepared for when an eclipse was forecast to take place. The 'king' would be dressed in the real king's clothing and treated like the king, even being paired with a young woman as his 'queen'. The real king would retreat into hiding until the eclipse had passed: in a gruesome twist, the stand-in couple were killed before the real king returned to take over his duties once more. On 1 August 1133, Henry I left England on a ship bound for Normandy. As he travelled, a solar eclipse took place on 2 August, and this was seen as a bad omen, predicting that Henry would never return to England alive. He died in France in 1135, heralding a period of chaos and unrest for England.

Due to a variety of negative connotations, many people therefore chose to hide away when an eclipse was taking place. One Hindu belief was that water was the safest place to be during an eclipse, and the very safest water of all was the Ganges River due to its sacred state. In south-western Alaska, there was a belief that during an eclipse, an unclean essence fell to earth. This was said to cause great harm if it landed on utensils or plates and dishes that people might use and eat from, and sickness would result. Therefore at the start of an eclipse, to avoid disaster, dishes, pots and other receptacles were turned upside down so they could not be infected.

WHY THE SUN AND THE MOON LIVE IN THE SKY

Have you ever wondered how the sun and moon came to be in the sky? You might think that they have always been there but, according to this tale from southern Nigeria, many, many years ago, the sun and moon actually lived together right here on earth.

Back then, one of the sun's greatest friends was the water; but although the sun would visit the water often, the water never returned these calls. The sun accepted this for a while, but finally asked the water why it was he never came to visit him in his house. The water then told him that he couldn't visit because the sun's house was not large enough for him to do so; if he came with all of his people, he would fill the sun's house and drive him out.

Seeing how this upset his friend, the water then had an idea. If he really wanted the water to visit him, he told the sun, the sun would need to build a large compound, as huge and vast as he could manage. This was absolutely essential if the plan were to succeed: the water's people were many, and required a great deal of space.

The sun agreed to this readily, and promised to build a huge area as the water had told him. With the deal struck, the sun made his way back home to the moon, his wife, and told her what he had promised. True to his word, the sun set to work the very next day in building the enclosure that would hold the water and all of his people when they came to visit. Eager to finally have his friend in his home, the sun worked very hard and very quickly. Finally it was finished and the sun didn't delay, inviting the water to visit him the very next day.

The water, still a little cautious, arrived at the appointed time. He called to the sun, asking him if it was safe for him to enter. The confident sun called back in the affirmative, telling his friend to come in. Convinced, the water entered, starting to flow into the enclosure. The fish and all the animals of the water went with him, pouring into the space. It was not long at all before the water was at knee-height, and the water checked again with the sun whether it was still safe. The sun assured him that yes, it was all right, and so more water entered.

More and more water flowed in, and soon it was as high as a man. Again, the water asked the sun whether more of his people could come in. The sun and the moon, not knowing what they were agreeing to, again answered yes, and the water became a steady flow, filling every space available. The sun and moon soon found themselves perched precariously at a great height, as there was no longer enough space for them anywhere else. Even this did not stop the sun from agreeing when the water asked if more of his people could come in! Thus encouraged, the water kept on coming and coming, until, lo and behold, the very roof was covered in a watery deluge.

What happened to the sun and the moon? With no other choice, they fled upwards into the sky, to the very places where we are accustomed to seeing them today.

HINA:
The Woman in the Moon

According to Polynesian belief, the goddess Hina lives in the moon. In some versions of her tale, Hina and the maidens who worked with her made the finest kappa cloth known to humankind. Day in, day out, the busy Hina was never still; as well as the cloth, she braided mats from the leaves from the hala tree, giving them to members of the household to sleep on, and she also used nuts from the kukui trees to make torches, which in turn were used to illuminate the homes of the highest-ranking of families.

Hina worked so long and so hard, that finally she had enough of labouring among the mortals of the earth. Her own family brought her little comfort: her husband was lazy and did nothing for himself, her sons were troublesome and disorderly, and she found she had little to stay for. So Hina decided to escape. Looking upwards, she spied the tempting path of the rainbow and hatched a plan. She would use it to take her to the sun, where she could rest and escape from her troubles.

Early the next morning, Hina began to climb the rainbow, armed with her calabash packed with her most treasured belongings. But the higher she went, the hotter she became, the strong, powerful rays of the sun beating down upon her so relentlessly that after a time she found she could barely crawl her way along. Still Hina did not give up, but every fraction higher she went it got hotter and hotter. It was no use; she was nearly on fire, and in so much pain that she finally abandoned her attempt, sliding back down the rainbow to the earth once more.

Away from the scorching heat, Hina recovered her strength. When the moon rose and night fell, she decided to try again. This time, though, she would climb up to the moon instead to find the

rest she craved. Alas for Hina, she was spotted as she started her new journey, and her husband called to her, telling her not to leave the earth.

Hina would not be dissuaded, telling him that she would go to the moon, who would be her new husband. So saying, she carried on, climbing higher with each moment. Not to be outsmarted, her husband followed, running towards her. She was almost too high, but he jumped and managed to catch her foot. The desperate Hina shook him off, but not without paying a painful price. As her husband fell downwards he broke her leg, the bottom part of it coming away in his hands.

Crying out the strongest incantations she could muster, Hina passed through the stars. The powers of the night hastened to her aid as she was lifted through the darkness until she at last found herself at the door of the moon.

Throughout everything, Hina had kept tight hold of her calabash, and with it she finally limped into the moon. There Hina found her forever home ... and peace at last. When the moon is full, it is said that if you look up you can see Hina there, calabash still by her side. The board where she beat her cloth can also be seen down on earth, turned into a stone at the foot of the fish head-shaped headland known as Kauiki.

MAN, RABBIT, OR JACK AND JILL?
The Many Faces of the Moon

A peculiar trait of humankind is the habit of seeing identifiable images in otherwise random patterns or shapes. This *pareidolia* as it is known is very common in relation to the moon, and for thousands of years people have been envisaging all manner of figures and characters when they gaze upwards at the earth's only natural satellite. What exactly is seen on the face of the moon – in reality the dark seas and lighter highlands of the lunar landscape – varies from culture to culture, and ideas range from a man, to a hare, to King Mohammed V of Morocco. A splendid array of tales and explanations have sprung forth in support of these ideas: just who do *you* think lives on the moon?

The Man in the Moon

One of the most common interpretations of the face of the moon in Europe is that it looks like a man. Old and wizened, the Man in the Moon is generally seen as bent over, often carrying a load of sticks upon his back. The idea of there being a Man in the Moon is an ancient one, dating back thousands of years, with many differing suggestions regarding the man's identity and just how he came to be on the moon in the first place.

A popular theme is that the man serves as a warning to others, a cautionary tale not to follow his bad example. In a tale from Germany, the man was cutting sticks for fuel in the forest one

Sunday and, after he had finished, slung them over his shoulder on his staff. On the way home, he met a man dressed in Sunday best heading in the direction of church. 'Do you not know that you should be in church as it is Sunday?' the man demanded of him. Unimpressed, the old man just laughed, saying that Sunday was just the same as any other day to him. Well, said the younger man, in that case he could carry his bundle forever! With that, he was banished to the moon, a reminder and warning to all who might be tempted to break the Sabbath. Some link the tale to the story in the Bible in the book of Numbers that relates how a man was caught gathering sticks on the Sabbath and was sentenced by Moses to be stoned, although there is no mention there of the moon.

In some versions, the man is guilty of stealing from a neighbour and is likewise punished. In North Frisia, Germany, a man was guilty of stealing cabbages on Christmas Eve from his neighbours. He was caught in the act and as punishment the people used magic to send him up to the moon. In another version it was willow boughs that he stole, but the result was the same. According to a Dutch tale, the man was caught stealing vegetables.

Another idea with German origins says that there are both a man and a woman in the moon. The man was guilty of laying thorns and brambles across the path to stop people getting to church on a Sunday. The woman was not much better, as she broke the Sabbath by making butter on that day. Both were banished upwards to the moon, the man still seen holding his thorny bundle and the woman with her butter tub.

In Malaysia, the man is busy braiding bark to make a fishing line. If he completes the line, he will use it to catch up everything that is upon the earth, a disaster that must be avoided at all costs. Fortunately, there is a rat that gnaws at the line so that it cannot be finished, and a cat that chases the rat in turn, making sure between them that balance is maintained and disaster averted.

Although seeing a Man in the Moon is very common in the northern hemisphere, he doesn't make an appearance in stories from the southern hemisphere. This is because the moon is seen differently depending on which hemisphere you are in, and thus the markings and lightness and shade upon the moon's surface are perceived in a different way.

The Fox

In Peru it is said that the animal on the face of the moon is actually a fox. Many, many years ago, at a time when it was common for animals to talk, Fox had a dream: more than anything, he longed to visit the moon. He watched it and gazed at it, and day by day his desire to go there grew and grew. Finally he confided his wish to his friend, Mole, and explained his plan to get there.

Mole, more interested in eating worms than in thoughts of what went on in the sky, was not very keen on the idea, but Fox convinced him with the promise of fresh moon worms, and so the pair went about carrying out Fox's plan. According to Fox, all they needed to do was fashion a rope out of grass, hook it over the moon when it was in its crescent form, and then use it to climb upwards. It sounded so simple, and the pair worked hard to braid grass into a rope long enough, they thought, to reach the moon. With the rope finally completed, then came the wait: they waited patiently as the moon passed through its phases, until at last they were rewarded with the sight of the crescent moon in the sky, the hooked end beckoning them enticingly. How close they were, thought Fox, to getting there!

But, alas, it was not as easy as he had first thought. Try as they might, they could not throw that rope high enough to hook over the end of the moon. Time and time again the rope went so high, but then crashed back down to earth before them. The disappointment! Mole would have welcomed giving up at this point, but Fox would not be dissuaded even then. At a loss, they went to ask Bear to help them. Bear could climb higher than any animal, but even when at the top of the highest tree, he couldn't quite reach to hook the rope over the moon as they wanted. The same went for Llama – although he could climb to the top of the highest mountain, it just wasn't quite high enough. Finally they asked Condor and, lo and behold, the plan finally worked and the magnificent bird managed to hook the rope securely over the end of the moon.

Making sure to secure the other end to a tree, Fox and Mole then started to climb. Fox went ahead, but Mole was more hesitant, lamenting how dizzy he felt if he looked down. Fox admonished his friend and told him not to look down but to keep going, and up, up, up they went, ever closer to reaching their goal.

Now there are different versions of what happened next. Some say that Mole, in his nervousness, slipped and was caught by Condor, who then flew him back down to earth. There the other animals teased him, and Mole hid in the ground where he lives to this day. In another version, as they were climbing, Parrot came to jeer at Mole, saying that he would never make it all the way to the moon. Mole retorted that Parrot was just jealous that he was not going to the moon with them. This angered Parrot and he pecked at the rope until it broke, sending Mole falling back towards the ground. Luckily Condor caught him and brought him back to earth safely.

As for Fox, in all accounts, he continued on upwards, safely reaching the moon, where he can still be seen to this day.

The Water Carriers

Some see two children in the shapes on the moon's face. In the 13th-century Icelandic *Younger Edda* written by Snorri Sturluson, there is reference to two such children. Named Hjúki (meaning 'the one returning to health' in Old Norse) and Bil (meaning either 'moment' or 'instant'), the pair were on their way from the well Byrgir, carrying a bucket between them on the pole known as Simul on their shoulders. Máni the moon god, spying them, took them up from the earth to be with him, and that is where they are now, following him through the heavens. Based on this, it is said by some that the figures seen on the moon are none other than these two children.

Very little else is known of the elusive Hjúki and Bil, as they are not mentioned outside of the *Younger Edda*, though Bil is mentioned later on in the same text as a minor deity, along with the sun goddess Sól. It has been suggested that the pair might represent the phases of the moon, but the more accepted theory is that the two children are an explanation for the craters and shapes on the moon's surface as seen from the earth.

There is some speculation that Snorri took the idea of the children from a now unknown folk tale, or that he invented them altogether. Due to the similarity in names, the water-carrying aspect of the story, and the hill, there is a theory that the two children are actually referenced in the popular English nursery rhyme, Jack and Jill.

There is another Siberian legend that tells of a young girl who is kidnapped by the moon when carrying a pitcher. She clings on to a willow bush in an attempt not to be taken, but to no avail; she can still be seen in the moon, clinging to the shrub.

The Toad

Out of all the animals seen in the moon, a toad or frog is one of the most common. The idea is particularly prevalent in China: this motif is recorded in the *I Ching*, or 'Book of Changes', from over 2,400 years ago.

There are many variations and differences in details to the tale, but the essential story involves a woman named Chang'e or Chang Er and her husband Archer Yi. Yi had obtained the herb or elixir of immortality from the Queen Mother of the West, but Chang'e took the herb for herself and consumed it, before floating off to the moon. In some versions Chang'e turned into a toad, and there she remains in that form.

In some tellings, Chang'e is beautiful yet vain and haughty, in stark contrast with her pious husband. Her punishment for stealing the elixir from him is twofold – not only is she banished, she also loses her greatly treasured beauty when she is transformed into a toad. There are other versions where the roles are reversed; it is the husband who is vain and arrogant, turning over time from a hero of the people into one of the worst tyrants imaginable. Desperate for the elixir so that he can be immortal, he will stop at nothing: knowing how dangerous it would be for a man such as her husband to have eternal life, Chang'e takes the elixir so that he cannot, and floats off to the moon, thwarting him as he tries to shoot arrows at her to bring her down.

The woman's original name was actually Heng'e, but this was changed to Chang'e after using the name Heng – meaning 'eternal' – became prohibited when a Han emperor used it in his title. Some believe that Chang'e is a moon goddess, but there is also an argument that she is the moon spirit itself: a toad in earlier versions of the story. It could be that the toad was the earliest creature or person to live in the moon in China.

According to some, Chang'e is not entirely alone in her lunar exile. There is the Jade Rabbit there to keep her company, pounding the very elixir she took in its pestle and mortar. There is also a woodcutter, doomed to forever hack at a cinnamon tree that heals each cut every time he makes one.

A toad is also associated with the moon in a tale attributed to the Sqelix or Salish from the Pacific coast of North America. Once there was a wolf in love with a toad, so obsessed with the toad that he followed her everywhere he could. The toad wasn't interested in the slightest, and hid from the wolf, leaving the bereft creature to pine alone. Wolf finally asked Moon to shine so he could find Toad, and Moon did so: the joyous wolf chased after the toad throughout the night once more. Poor Toad! She ran and ran and ran and was nearly caught, but with one last burst of energy she leapt as high into the sky as she could. She reached the moon, and is there even today.

Another tale from the Sqelix people tells of how the moon invited all the people to a great feast. Toad, offended when she was told there was nowhere for her to sit, went home and made it rain heavily. Eventually there was nowhere dry for people to shelter, until they saw a light and went to Toad's house. Finding it dry, they crammed inside, and Toad leapt onto Moon's face. Try as they might, people could not pull her away, and the marks from Toad are said to still be on the moon's face today for all to see.

The Hare

Another common idea is that a rabbit or hare lives on the moon, a motif found in several different cultures. The Sea of Tranquillity is seen as the rabbit's head, while the seas of Fertility and Nectar are the ears.

In a story in the Buddhist *Sasa-jātaka*, the hare had three friends: the otter, jackal and monkey. Hare told his companions how it was good to give alms, and how, on the forthcoming fast day, they should give food to any beggar who asked for it. When the next day came, the deity Sakka – ruler of the Trāyastriṃśa heaven, and a protector of Buddhism according to Buddhist belief – came down to earth disguised as an old man, and asked for food to test them all. Otter, Jackal and Monkey all readily gave food that they had to hand, but Hare, having nothing to gather but grass, knew this would not do, and offered himself upon a fire for Sakka to eat. For his faithfulness, Sakka did not allow the hare to perish, but plucked him from the flames and set him in the moon. In some versions, he used the essence extracted from squeezing the mountain to draw the image of the faithful hare on the moon for all to see. There are other very similar stories about a self-sacrificing hare in other cultures, with different animals being listed as his friends.

In a tale from Sri Lanka, Buddha was lost in a wood. Hare offered to help him find his way, but Buddha said he was hungry and poor and could not pay him for his services. Hare immediately offered himself to eat; when Buddha made a fire, Hare threw himself onto it, but Buddha, using his powers, saved the selfless creature and sent him to the moon where he is today. There is a similar tale in Japan, where the rabbit is known as Tsuki no Usagi, and the Man in the Moon comes down to earth disguised as a beggar. The other animals present him with food, but the rabbit, with only grass to offer, sacrifices himself on the fire for the beggar,

who then transforms into his original form and takes the rabbit up to live with him in recognition of his selflessness. This is a popular Japanese tale, and often told to children in September, at the time of the Harvest Moon and the Mid-Autumn Festival.

In a different vein, according to a tale from South Africa, the hare is responsible for the fact that humankind is doomed to die. Moon sent Hare down to tell people that just as she, the moon, 'died' when she faded away each month, only to return again, so would humankind. But Hare did not deliver the message correctly; instead, the flighty creature told people only that they would die. When Moon found out what Hare had done she was so angry she attacked him with a hatchet, intending to split him in two. She only succeeded in splitting his lip, however. Hare, angry in turn, lashed out with his claws, scarring Moon's face, which can still be seen in the dark shapes on the moon today.

According to Aztec mythology, the gods gathered to appoint a new sun after the fourth sun came to an end. The choice was between two gods: proud, handsome Tecciztecatl and lowly, ugly Nanahuatzin, and the one to become the sun had to throw themselves into the fire. At the last moment, Tecciztecatl hesitated, leaving Nanahuatzin to make the sacrifice first. Recovering himself, Tecciztecatl then followed, but this then left a situation where there were two suns. The remaining gods threw a rabbit at Tecciztecatl, leaving the mark on his face and making him much dimmer than Nanahuatzin. Tecciztecatl could only be seen at night, and thus became the moon.

THE MORNING STAR AND THE EVENING STAR:
A Romanian Tale

O nce upon a time there was an emperor and empress who longed to be blessed with a child. They stopped at nothing to achieve their desire, consulting with witches and wizards and others with such skills, but to no avail. The desperate couple, with no further recourse, gave themselves over to fasting, praying and the giving of alms to the poor, in the hope that this might do some good for their plight. To the empress's delight, their efforts were not in vain: one night she dreamed that the Lord himself appeared to her, bringing the news she longed to hear. He promised her that she and the emperor would be blessed with a child unlike any other, but only if they would follow certain instructions. According to the empress's dream, the emperor was to take a hook and line to the brook; when he caught a fish, the empress was to prepare it herself and eat it, and this would ensure she was with child.

Overjoyed, the empress woke her husband and told him what had occurred. The emperor wasted no time and leapt from his bed, and they hurried to the brook and did as instructed. The couple waited with bated breath, but did not have long to wait: a short while later the cork started to bob. The line was pulled in, and to their amazement and great joy, at the end was a huge golden fish.

The empress continued to follow the instructions from her dream, and soon had the fish prepared and cooked. The pair ate it, and the empress immediately knew that she was indeed with child as she had been promised. Unbeknown to the royal couple, however, when clearing the table, a maidservant spied a fish bone left on the empress's plate. Giving in to temptation, she sucked it, curious to know how the dish from her mistress's table tasted.

Time passed, and the empress gave birth to a baby boy, perfectly angelic in every way. That very same night, the maidservant who had sucked the fish bone also had a boy: and guess what? The two children were so completely identical, that no one could tell them apart. The prince was named Busujok, the maid's son Siminok.

These two boys, so alike in looks, and bringing such joy to those around them, were each other's constant companions as they grew up. They learned together and played together and, as the years passed, grew into fine young men, charming, handsome, eloquent and brave. Still no one could tell the difference between them, and one was often mistaken for the other.

This difficulty plagued the empress, as even she very often could not tell her own son from the other youth. One day, when the men decided to go out hunting, the anxious mother called her son to her; stroking his hair, she secretly knotted two locks together, before sending him on his way with his friend.

The energy and enjoyment of these two young men knew no bounds. They played in the fields, watched bees and butterflies dart through the air, gathered flowers and, when finally starting to tire, drank water from thirst-quenching springs. The pair then ventured into the woods, gazing around in astonishment at the vast beauty of the forest around them. As they wandered they discussed what they would hunt, and quickly agreed that they would only hunt wild beasts, leaving the birds and other animals to go free. It had been a long, wonderful, yet intense day, and the prince was suddenly overcome with tiredness, too weary to stand a moment longer. He lay down, placing his head in Siminok's lap, asking him to stroke his hair.

It was in doing so that Siminok came across the knotted locks; exclaiming in surprise, he alerted the prince to the fact that his hair had been tied together. The prince was very confused, and did not like this discovery. He was so confounded that he declared his intention to go out into the wide world, as he could not fathom why his mother had tied his hair so.

Siminok tried to dissuade him, saying that the empress would not have done so for any evil cause and must have some innocent explanation. The prince would not be talked around, however, and he did not back down. Busujok bid his closest friend and brother farewell, giving him a handkerchief. He told him that if he ever saw three drops of blood on the handkerchief, then Siminok would know that he, the prince, was dead.

Embracing, they parted, each going their separate ways, Siminok returning to the palace to break the news to the empress and emperor. The poor empress was inconsolable, weeping and wringing her hands with great grief. The presence of Siminok, looking so much like her son, was some comfort, but that did not last. Siminok, glancing at the handkerchief one day, noticed three drops of blood upon it. Declaring that this meant his brother was dead he took off in search of the prince.

On and on he travelled, across fields and through forests and beyond. Finally Siminok reached a small hut, where he discovered an old woman. The woman informed him that Busujok was now the son of the local emperor, married to the princess.

With this news, Siminok made his way to the emperor's palace with all haste. As he approached, however, the princess saw him, and of course mistook him for her own husband, Busujok. Siminok told her that he was not the prince but in fact his friend, and that, upon hearing that he was dead, had come to find out what had happened. The princess was not convinced; she was certain that Siminok was indeed her husband and was playing a trick on her. Siminok tried again to tell her that he was not her husband, and finally declared that the Lord himself would reveal the truth: the sword that hung on a nail nearby would scratch the one of them who was wrong in their belief.

Of course, the sword cut the princess: she accordingly believed him, and accepted him as a guest. During the course of his inquiries, Siminok discovered that Busujok had gone out hunting, but he had not come home. Siminok wasted no time in taking a horse and some hounds and set off after him, riding on and on across the kingdom. At the forest, he encountered the Wood Witch. She ran away when she saw him, but he gave chase, finally catching up with her at the foot on a tall tree. The witch fled upwards, hoping to be safe in the protective branches.

Siminok was not easily dissuaded, and simply set up camp at the foot of the tree, made a fire and started to eat; his greyhounds settled nearby, accepting the occasional bite of food. Eventually the witch complained of being cold, and when Siminok suggested she join him by the fire, she expressed fear of the dogs. He told her they would do her no harm and she wavered, finally telling him to take a strand of her hair and tie the dogs up with it. Siminok agreed but instead put the hair in the fire. The witch, suspicious, asked if he had burned the hair, but Siminok denied the fact, saying he had done as she requested. The witch believed him and came down from her refuge, moving closer to the fire. When she told him she was hungry, Siminok asked what she would want to eat; in an expected moment of treachery, she told him she would eat him. Siminok was ready for her, however, and let the hounds go to tear her apart.

The witch, knowing she was caught, cried for him to call them off, promising that she would give the prince back if he did so. Siminok quickly called off his hounds, and the witch, true to her word, swallowed three times. To his amazement, up came Busujok, along with his horse and dogs too. Once they were free, Siminok set his hounds on the witch again, and they tore her to pieces.

After her demise, the prince related how he had been asleep, and Siminok in turn told him of what had occurred during his absence. Unfortunately, the suspicious prince believed that the princess had turned her affections to his brother instead, and nothing would dissuade him of this notion. In his madness, the prince declared that each of the brothers should cover their horses' eyes, mount, and let the horse carry each of them where they chose.

Siminok agreed, and the two duly bound their horses' eyes and their own. After a time, Busujok heard a groan; the prince halted his horse and freed his eyes. He looked all around for his brother, but there was no sign of him: alas, he had fallen into the spring and drowned.

Busujok made his way home and interrogated his wife on the story that Siminok had told him. She of course told him the exact same tale and, just to make extra sure, the prince told the sword to scratch whichever of them was wrong. It did so, scratching his own middle finger.

Too late, the prince regretted his jealousy and suspicion. He lamented and pined, overwhelmed by the weight of his grief at the loss of his dear brother. He could not, he decided, live without him any longer: he bound his eyes and those of his horse, before setting out to the forest where Siminok had died. Once there, the horse fell into the very same spring, and Busujok likewise drowned.

At that very moment, the emperor's son Busujok appeared in the sky as the morning star, and Siminok the maid's son appeared as the evening star. And that is how they came to be.

THE SEVEN SISTERS:
Orion and the Pleiades

There are perhaps no two arrangements of stars that have more captured the imagination throughout history than the Pleiades and Orion. Tales and superstitions regarding them both abound, with striking and intriguing similarities between disparate cultures and lands.

The Pleiades asterism consists of around 3,000 hot, blue, relatively young stars, about 115–125 million years old. To the average, well-sighted person, however, today only six are visible to the naked eye. Considered one of the most stunning sights in the night sky, the Pleiades can be found on the shoulder of Taurus the Bull.

The Pleiades was one of the earliest asterisms to be named: mentioned by Ancient Greek writers Homer and Hesiod, they are also one of the few asterisms outside of the Zodiac mentioned in the Old Testament, and the stars are also referenced in the New Testament. The oldest symbolic representation of the Pleiades is believed to be found on the Nebra Sky Disc; this artefact, discovered in Germany and thought to have been made around 1600 BCE, shows six stars arranged around a seventh, which are believed to represent the Pleiades. Archaeological evidence also speaks to the important role the Pleiades played in many cultures, and it is believed that the Temple of the Sun in Mexico, Egypt's Great Pyramid and the Parthenon in Athens, Greece, were among those monuments aligned with the Pleiades or built with them in mind.

With strong links to the phases of the agricultural year, in many cultures the rising and setting of the Pleiades has been used to mark important stages in the calendar. For many of the pastoralist groups in South Africa, the Pleiades are known by various names that translate to the 'Digging' or 'Ploughing' stars. When they first appear in the sky, it is seen as the signal for hoeing to begin, ready for the agricultural year ahead. To some of the indigenous groups of Borneo, Southeast Asia, the disappearance and return of the Pleiades each year marked the passing of the seasons and determined their agricultural pursuits; likewise in Peru, the appearance of the Pleiades also governed the crops and harvest. According to belief in both Belarus and Lithuania, it was time to sow corn after the asterism had risen. The Pleiades were also relied upon by many indigenous groups across America, a connection strengthened by the fact that the stars themselves were thought to look like a heap of seeds: they were actually called 'the seeds' by the A:shiwi of New Mexico. Some Japanese nomadic cultures used the celestial movements of various stars and bodies to judge when to move and where to find food; the Pleiades – or Subaru – was an especially important asterism in this regard.

Unsurprisingly then, the Pleiades were also linked with the ability to foretell the weather, especially where rain seasons were concerned. According to a Swahili proverb from South Africa, 'If the Digging stars set in sunny weather, they rise in rain, if they set in rain, they rise in sunny weather.' The Khoikhoi of South Africa used the Pleiades to forecast the start of the rain season, while the Tapirapé people of Brazil believe that when the Pleiades disappeared it is a sign that the rainy season is coming to an end. The Pleiades were generally used for marking the passage of time: for the South African AmaXhosa, they marked each fresh year of adulthood for men of the tribe. For several Indigenous Australian groups, the heliacal rising of the Pleiades marks the beginning of winter.

The Pleiades have also long had navigational links, used in particular by sailors to find their way across the wide dark seas. To reflect this, in Ancient Greece they were known as the sailing stars, and in Germany today they are still known as *Schiffahrts Gestirn* – Sailors' Stars – along with their official name of Plejaden.

In some Polynesian cultures, this asterism also played an important navigational role, as people used the stars to guide their journeys during the night.

But who exactly were the Pleiades and how did the stars get their name? According to Greek mythology, the Pleiades were the beautiful daughters of Atlas and the nymph Pleione. Orion the Hunter fell deeply in love with the girls and wouldn't take no for an answer, pursuing them relentlessly wherever they went. With no help forthcoming from their father, who was condemned to hold up the earth until the end of time, the maidens despaired. Zeus, however, took pity on them and heard their pleas; he turned the girls into doves, and they flew up into the sky where they became the stars of the Pleiades. Even now Orion hasn't ceased his pursuit; he can be seen today, still chasing them across the night sky. In another, more sinister, version of the origin tale, the sisters committed suicide out of sadness for their father, and were then placed in the sky.

This idea that the stars represent seven or six people, usually sisters or young women, is one of the most popular and common explanations across the globe for the Pleiades. According to a tale of the O-non-dowa-gah or Seneca people of North America, the Pleiades were seven young sisters, transformed into stars because they stayed too long when visiting a magical fountain. A Prussian tale has the Pleiades as the wife and daughters of a tyrannical husband who turns into a cuckoo. In Belarus, the stars are known as Siem Malciev, 'seven men'.

One of the most intriguing aspects of the Pleiades is the wealth of tales suggesting there were once seven stars clearly visible to the naked eye and that one of these stars at some point in history ceased to shine brightly enough to be seen, leaving the six that we see today. Some scholars believe that the strong similarities between such tales from Europe and Australia suggest that they originated from before the time when the ancestors of both cultures migrated out of Africa, which would date tales of the missing star to before 100,000 BCE. This detail features in stories

across such disparate nations and cultures that it is very probable one of the stars used to shine more brightly at some point than it did later, and missing Pleiades stories are found in African, Asian, European, Native American and Indigenous Australian cultures.

According to Greek mythology, it was the sister Merope who left the group: she felt such disgrace after marrying a mortal that she withdrew from her sisters. Another tale holds that it was Electra who vanished, hiding her face in grief when the city of Troy fell. In the belief of Indigenous groups in Australia there are many variations on what happened to the missing Pleiad, usually involving one, or sometimes even two, sisters either being abducted, dying or going into hiding.

In a tale from the Mono of Central California, six women discovered onions while out picking herbs one day. They tasted them and enjoyed them so much that they ate as many of the onions as they could find, only returning home when it grew dark. Their husbands – returning from a day hunting cougar – were not impressed with the smell, and made the women sleep outside. Despite this, the next day when the men went out hunting, the women went out again to eat more onions as they had enjoyed them so much. The men returned home angry and tired; they had not managed to catch any cougar, they said, as they smelled like the onions and scared away the prey.

A week passed in such a fashion, with the wives eating onions and the men catching nothing. The men were increasingly cross because of this, and the women were fed up and angry too because they could not sleep well outside in the cold. On the seventh day, the women took ropes with them when they went out. Resting at the top of a large rock nearby, they decided to leave their husbands. One of the women whispered a secret word, and then threw her rope straight up into the sky. Like magic, it hooked over a cloud, with the two ends hanging down towards the women. The others tied their own ropes to it, and as they sang a special song, their ropes began to swing, taking them up into the sky. The men returned in time to see them and were instantly sorry; they too used magic and started to follow their wives up into the sky. The women were not happy with this, and shouted at them to stop – they did so, just a little way behind them. The women were turned into stars – six bright ones and one fainter one, the little girl of one of the wives. The men are also still there to this day, represented in the constellation of Taurus.

Another popular motif is that the Pleiades represent a mother hen and her chicks. This idea can be found across a large portion of central, western and southern Europe, West Africa, the Sudan, north-east India and south-east Africa. According to some indigenous groups of Borneo, the stars are six chicks, followed by their invisible mother. Once upon a time there were seven chicks, but one went down to the earth and was given food. This greatly angered the mother hen, and she threatened to destroy both her chicks and the people on earth. In Hungary, the stars are also said to be a hen and chicks, and likewise to the Imohag, a Berber group of the Sahara, they are also chickens. In a similar vein, the names for the Pleiades among several groups located in northern Russia all mean 'nest of eggs' or 'of a wild duck' or 'flock of ducks'. In Thailand, the stars are called Dao Luk Kai, the 'Chicken Family Stars'.

In a tale from Croatia, there was a church that was threatened with destruction by its enemies. In the dead of night, the intruders were creeping up on their target when the hen, Kvoĉka, flew down from her tree outside the church, screaming and flying about to alert the people of the impending attack. The church was saved, and its would-be destroyers fled, but could not be found. Again, Kvoĉka saved the day: the people heard her clucking and followed the sound to the place where the enemies were concealing themselves, and they were apprehended. At that moment, someone happened to look up at the sky, and noticed that a group of stars there looked like Kvoĉka, and so they have been named ever since.

Another popular idea is that the constellation represents a sieve in the night sky, with the stars being the holes in the sieve. This explanation for the Pleiades can be found in Western Ukraine, south-east Poland, the Balkans, Russia and Western Europe. In the Slutsk and Homiel regions of Belarus, the sieve was where souls were sifted, the good going to heaven, the bad to hell.

In some tales, the sieve is linked to Mary, mother of Jesus. In Poland, it is said that the three Magi left the sieve that they used to sift their horses' oats in Bethlehem, and Mary used it, then hung it in the sky. In Lithuania, Mary used the sieve to sift flour, but one day it went missing, stolen by the Devil. St Mark was charged with returning it, and he and the Devil got into a fight. The sieve was retrieved, but damaged beyond use, and Mary hung it in the sky. In the folklore of Lithuania and Latvia, the sieve was likewise also sometimes stolen from a sky god.

Other explanations for the Pleiades are varied and equally intriguing. A Polynesian tale tells how there was a star that shone so brightly in the sky that the god Tāne grew greatly jealous. He threw Aldebaran, another star, at it, and the star broke into six pieces, each in turn becoming its own star. In the Near East and North Africa, the Pleiades are known by the Persian-Arabic word *soyraya*, meaning 'chandelier' or 'cluster of lamps', while to the Söl'kup, native to Siberia, they were hare's droppings. In Russia, Ukraine, Bulgaria, Hungary and the Volga Region, the asterism is seen as a beehive.

What then of Orion, the constellation so closely linked to the Pleiades in many myths and legends? Orion is likewise mentioned in the Old Testament, and the Ancient Greek writings of Homer and Hesiod. Who was Orion, and why is his constellation so important? According to most sources, he was Boeotian by birth, a giant and a hunter. Tales of his birth vary: according to some sources he was the son of Poseidon the sea god, and Euryale, and had the ability to walk on the waves of the sea. In another tale, when three gods visited King Hyrieus of Thrace, they were impressed by the king's hospitality and granted him a wish. He wished for children, so the three gods urinated on the hide of an ox that the king had sacrificed, the skin was buried, and from it was born Urion – later known as Orion. Although far from one of the largest constellations – Orion is only 26th in line – it is the constellation recognized most by people, his club, lion skin, belt or girdle, and sword easily located in the night sky. Unlike some constellations, Orion is visible across the globe.

Orion's pursuit of the Pleiades has a long history; Hesiod, circa 700 BCE, refers to his chase of the ill-fated sisters across the sky. There is some dispute over who exactly Orion is chasing after, however; Hyginus said that it was actually Pleione, the mother of the Pleiades sisters, that he was chasing.

In some traditional Indigenous Australian tales, most cultures have associated Orion with a man, or a group of young men, and there are many stories centring around Orion trying to catch the Pleiades. In Arnhem Land, northern Australia, there were stories that portrayed the Pleiades as the partners of the men who make up Orion. In New South Wales and Victoria, the girls of the Pleiades make music, and in some stories the boys of Orion dance at night to it.

In one Greek tale, the great hunter set his sights on marriage to Merope, daughter of King Oenopion of Chios. Orion carried out many tasks to help the king, including ridding the area of beasts, but the king did not really want his daughter married to one such as Orion, and continually put off the day that the pair would marry. One night, drunk and out of control, Orion forced himself upon Merope; when the king discovered this, he asked his father, the god Dionysius, for help. The god obliged, enlisting the help of the satyrs to put Orion into unconsciousness, and with him in this state, the king blinded the hunter who had done his daughter such wrong. Orion sought help from the god Hephaestus for his condition, and was told that he needed to travel to the place where the sun rises, and to let the sun bathe his afflicted eyes. With the god's assistant as his guide, Orion went where he was bid and regained his sight: seeking revenge, he went after the king, but he was hidden underground and Orion could not reach him.

After a colourful and varied life, there are several different versions of how Orion met his end. According to one tale, he died at the hands of Artemis, goddess of the hunt, in punishment for raping one of her handmaidens. In another, Orion and Artemis were lovers, and the hunter sought to marry her. Apollo, Artemis's brother, was not happy with this, and came up with a scheme. He bet the proud goddess that she would not be able to hit the target he indicated far off in the sea. She took aim and fired, hitting the target true, only to learn that it had been Orion's head, bobbing in the water as he swam. In another, it was Orion's own boasting that brought about his death; he had bragged that he would hunt all the beasts on earth, and this was displeasing to Gaia, Mother Earth, and so she sent a scorpion to slay him and remove the threat. Whatever the cause of his death, Orion was placed in the stars where we still see him today.

Interestingly, the constellation of Orion has links with dismemberment in various myths across the globe. At Orion's right shoulder is the bright star with a reddish glow, Alpha Orionis or Betelgeuse, the second brightest within the constellation. In Arabic, its name is said to mean 'shoulder' or 'armpit of the giant' or 'central one'. To the Taulipang of northern Brazil, the constellation was a man called Zilikawai, and his wife hacked off his leg – the shoulder is seen as a leg as the constellation appears sideways. There is a similar tale told by the Warao of the Orinoco delta, who also say it is a leg, this time from a man named Nohi-Abassi. To the North American Lakota, Betelgeuse is also a limb, an arm of a chief, ripped off as a punishment.

According to one theory, Orion actually used to represent the Greek hero, Heracles. According to the Sumerians, Orion was Gilgamesh, fighting a giant bull – Taurus. Gilgamesh was the Sumerian version of Heracles. According to Egyptians, Orion's belt marked the resting place of the soul of the god Osiris. In a story from the Indigenous Australian group the Yolngu, the three stars that make up Orion's 'belt' represent three brothers in their canoe. They were blown up into the sky by the Sun-Woman as a punishment for violating the law when they ate a king-fish, their totem animal.

HOW THE MILKY WAY CAME TO BE

There are many tales from folklore and legend that attempt to explain the existence of the Milky Way, that winding, twisting galaxy in which our solar system is found. According to this story from South Africa, it is not made from stars at all, but from embers and ashes.

Many, many years ago, when it was night time, there was no light whatsoever in the sky, and the world was plunged into darkness at the end of each day. In time, however, resourceful humankind learned how to make fire, and they used it to bring light and warmth to themselves during the long dark-filled hours.

One night, a young girl sat before her wood fire, playing with the ashes as she warmed herself there. Taking some of the ashes in her hands, she cast them upwards into the air, watching them dance and swirl prettily, floating away into the air above. As she watched them go, the girl added more wood, stirring the fire to keep it going and making bright sparks dance and waft into the air after the ashes. How beautiful they looked! Hanging in the air, the sparks formed a bright road made from, it seemed, diamonds and silver, sparkling bright for all to see.

Called by some the Milky Way and by others the Stars' Road, it is still there today as splendid as ever, reminding us of the girl who threw those ashes and sparks up into the sky – a pathway of light shining in the darkness.

SOARING SOULS AND SHOOTING STARS:
Star Superstitions from Around the World

The enduring habit of humankind to attach meaning to signs and occurrences stretches back into the mists of time. When it comes to superstitious belief surrounding stars, it is tantalizingly apparent that such beliefs and ideas regarding the significance of the stars are shared across the globe.

Shooting Stars

Spotting a meteor, or shooting or falling star as they are commonly known, is a time-honoured pastime. Interpreted in many different ways, it is widely believed that catching sight of a falling star as it streaks across the night sky is an omen of good things to come. As well as a general sign of good luck, spying a shooting star can also have a variety of more specific interpretations.

According to superstition in Kentucky, USA, if a falling star was seen, someone in the family would marry soon. In Montenegro, Serbia and Macedonia, a falling star could indicate the escape of a person from imprisonment or captivity. Upon seeing a star it was important not to draw attention to the fact in order to help the person stay free: instead, it was advised to either remain silent, or say, 'Behind the thorns, behind a bush hide!' According to the Yolngu people of Arnhem Land, Australia, a meteor was a sign to a family that a relative had arrived home safely.

Being lucky enough to see a falling star could also help with health concerns. According to Marcellus of Bordeaux, writing in 350CE, they could cure pimples. To be free of the affliction, one should observe a shooting star and then wipe a cloth over the spots; the pimples would then transfer to the cloth and your face would be clear. There was an important caveat, however: make sure not to touch your face with your hand, otherwise the spots would simply be transferred there instead. In another example of a cure, Pliny, in his *Natural History*, stated that if a corn or callus was cut when a star was falling, it would be quickly cured.

What actually is a shooting star? Although science now tells us that the phenomenon is caused by tiny specks of space dust burning up as they enter the earth's upper atmosphere, there are many other explanations to be found. According to Romanian belief, a falling star was actually an angel flying to help someone in need. People, being sinful, could not see them, and so only saw the star. According the Karajarri people of Western Australia, the night sky was a dome, made of hard rock or shell. Each star in turn was a nautilus shell, housing a living fish; a meteor was a dead fish falling from its shell. The Indigenous Australians near the Pennefather River, Queensland, believed that a falling star was the spirit of a woman watering yams to aid their growth.

Falling stars were not always viewed positively, however. A common belief was that a falling star signified either a death had occurred or was to happen soon. This was particularly the case if a shooting star was seen when at a sickbed or on the way to visit a sick person: one mother from Yorkshire, England, related how she knew her child was going to die because she saw a shooting star the night before they passed. A popular belief in Belarus held that it was a bad idea to look at falling stars on 5 February, as it would mean a death would follow soon after. In Russia it was also taboo to look at shooting stars on 5 March (20 Feb in the old Russian calendar) for similar reasons.

Meteors have also been associated with evil magic and spirits. According to the Tiwi of Australia's Northern Territory, the spirit of a falling star searches for living things to consume. It is told how one old woman placed infants in a bag tied about her neck to hide them from the eyes of these evil spirits. Another practice among some peoples was to kiss a baby on the forehead if they saw a meteor, so the child wouldn't be seen. In the Halliste region of Estonia, it was believed that a shooting star was caused when an old demon threw his hot stones high up into the sky. A particularly strange meteor spirit known for its malevolence, the Jubena, was found in Eastern Cape York Peninsula, Australia. It cooked eggs and burned them on the coals, and these were seen as falling stars. The spirit was known to hunt people down and tickle them to death. According to the Arrente people of Australia, mushrooms were fallen stars imbued with evil magic; because of this, they were considered taboo and not to be eaten.

According to belief in Ukraine, if looking at a falling star, be sure to say 'Amen' three times. This means when it lands it will solidify as rosin and be harmless. Otherwise it will transform into a devil, causing great harm to people in the area. In Bulgaria, the Kervanka, or Lazhi-kervan, is the name given to a bad star of evil spirits and disaster. People followed this star as they set off in the morning and often ended up dead, attacked by evil spirits on the road.

It is also very important to show a shooting star respect. According to Belarusian belief, you shouldn't laugh at a falling star, or it might burn down your house!

Wishing on a Star

Another popular star superstition is the practice of wishing on a star or shooting star in the hope that the wish will come true. A belief found across many places and cultures, it is not always as straightforward as just making a wish, and varying conditions could be attached. The most common and widespread caveat is that the wish must be made before the star is gone from sight in order for it to come true, a belief found in nearly all areas where this superstition is followed.

It is also sometimes said that the precise star you wish on is important. The most popular choice to wish on is the first star seen in the evening. This belief is captured in the now popular rhyme:

Starlight, star bright, first star I see tonight.
I wish I may, I wish I might, have the wish I wish tonight.

The position of the star when the wish is made is also said by some to be important – if the star is on the right-hand side, then good luck will follow and the wish will come true, but if it is on the left, then bad luck should be expected.

Some say that you should wish on a certain number of stars in order for your wish to come true; for instance, a belief recorded in mid-20th-century Swansea, Wales, held that counting nine stars on nine nights in a row would ensure that you got what you wanted.

What you did after making the wish was also important. Certain prohibitions were named in a collection of superstitions collected from a sample of US college students; these variously specified that after wishing you should not look at the star again until you see a specified number of others, that you should throw kisses to three other stars before speaking, or that you shouldn't speak until you are asked a question that you can answer 'yes' to.

In Russia, a shooting star was said to be an angel, on its way to collect a departed soul. They did not refuse wishes at that time, so it was a good time to make a wish; as long as you could still see the falling star, the wish was likely to come true. The speed the star flew at also indicated how quickly the wish would be granted: the faster the better!

Stars are also said to be able to predict what the future might hold. Some believe they can predict how many children you will have. Just hold a piece of cloth up and look towards the evening star; the number of little stars you see around it will predict the number of children.

Pointing at Stars

According to widespread belief, pointing at stars is a big no-no. Although the precise reason for this is not clear, there are several suggestions for why pointing at the stars is a really bad idea. A popular theory is that, according to ancient belief, the stars were actually gods up in the skies. To point at one could imply disrespect – and who would want to risk angering a god? This is linked to similar beliefs of how it is taboo to point at other celestial bodies, such as the moon or rainbows.

In Germany, it was a commonly held practice to bite one's finger after pointing at a star, potentially to avoid the star having to bite the persons finger. Biting the finger would, in theory, prevent it from falling off. Superstition in Estonia decrees against pointing at a star as it falls: if you do, you might find your finger starts to decay! It was also considered bad luck to count the stars in the sky, so pointing and counting might be doubly unlucky. In the mid-19th century in Derbyshire, England, children would dare each other to count the stars, with the belief that the counter would be struck down dead upon reaching a hundred.

As with every rule, there are some exceptions. According to lore in Kentucky, USA, if you want to find something you have lost, just count a hundred stars without counting the same one twice. Counting seven stars for seven nights in a row could help with finding love; according to superstition, the first potential partner you shake hands with will be your future spouse. Similarly, sleeping with a mirror under your pillow after counting nine stars for nine nights in a row will make you dream of the person you will marry.

Weather and Harvests

The behaviour of the stars is also said to influence or foretell the weather. Brightly twinkling stars in the sky might be a fabulous sight, but according to belief in Dalmatia, south Croatia, it could foretell heavy winds ahead. An eastern European belief likewise held that a falling star meant wind to come. It was also commonly believed that if a star falls, the next day would bring thunder. In Bulgaria, if the night was clear, with bright shining stars, it was a sign that the weather would soon break.

The stars also played a part in the success or otherwise of the harvest to come. In East Anglia, England, it was said that if the Evening Star – Venus – hung low during the summer months, with the first star of the Great Bear's (Ursa Major) tail above it in the sky, then it was best to prepare for a bad harvest. In Bulgaria, if the Pleiades constellation vanishes from the night sky before St Nicholas's Day comes around, this is a good sign: the next year will be fertile. According to belief from the Grodno region of Belarus, a shooting star that flares means a good harvest, though if the star falls and a stone also falls to the earth, then the harvest will be a bad one. In many Slavic cultures, a shooting star was seen as a portent of wind to come. A large number of meteors in a shower could be a bad omen, meaning that only one kind of grain would prosper that year and the others would fail. If the stone of the star fell into a person's garden then this was a bad sign; misfortune in general for the household and a bad harvest for the garden.

Passing Souls

There is a long-held connection between human souls and the stars. In Classical belief, when the world was created, the creator divided the left-over material into a number of souls equal to that of the stars in the heavens; each soul was assigned to a star. Those who lived a good life would, at its end, return to their star for a blessed existence, but it was a different story for those who did not learn the lessons they were supposed to during life: their soul would return again and again in lesser forms until they passed the test. The Ancient Greeks believed that shooting stars were falling or rising souls, depending on which way the star was going, and this belief held for centuries.

A very common belief even today is that a falling star is a soul either falling to earth or ascending into heaven. In some South Slavic and East Slavic areas, a falling star marked the death of the person it belonged to. In Bulgaria, when someone dies, the star that started to shine at their birth, will fall into their tomb. In 19th-century Yorkshire, it was believed that falling stars were the souls of babies coming down from heaven. Similarly, in Romania, stars were the souls of unbaptized children shining in the sky. To help the soul of the unbaptized child, it was important to cross yourself or give the soul a name to help it on its way. A common belief among many Indigenous groups in Australia was that a falling star was the spirit of someone who had died, falling from the sky. Some groups believed that if the sight of the star was accompanied by a loud crash, then it signified the death of a great medicine man.

The direction the star was travelling was sometimes said to be significant. If a star fell downwards, then it marked a death; if going upwards, then a birth had occurred. If a star fell towards the left, then the departed soul was that of a wicked person, and had gone straight to hell. In Belarusian belief, the sight of a falling star could mean that the deceased had not reached heaven, and their soul had returned to earth in order to put right the wrongs they had done in their previous life.

The star's direction could also signify *how* a person had died. In Belarus, if the star fell in a slanting direction then the person died a natural death, while if it fell fast and straight, they had been killed. A slowly falling star indicated that the deceased had been ill for a long time before their passing.

Some believe that the way a star fell was linked to the character of the person who had died. If it fell in a straight line then they had been an honest and good person during life. A jaggedly falling star, however, indicated that the individual had been unkind.

According to the Wardaman people of Australia, after death a person's spirit passed through a hole in the sky. There it would shine as a star, watched over by the Rock Cod star, Munin (Arcturus). When its time came, the spirit fell down to earth as a shooting star. Landing in a stream, the Rock Cod looked after it once more, until the spirit was united with its mother and reincarnated as her baby.

In Lithuania, it was believed that if the star had a tail, then it belonged to a rich person, whereas a simple star signified a person in a less healthy financial position. A large star could belong to a grown-up, while children had smaller stars.

Have you ever heard the phrase that someone must have been born under a lucky star, used about those who seem to have a charmed life with everything going their way, or those who rise to great heights? Equally, there are those who seem to be constantly suffering, experiencing mishap after mishap, with nothing going right. Although obviously not supported by fact, according to some, this might not be a coincidence, and there is a belief that the star someone was born under influences their entire personalities and life ahead. In Romanian belief, the star of an emperor, for instance, was bright and large – a *luceafar* – while a small, faint star signified a poorer, less-important individual. In Bulgaria, a sickly child is said to be of a weak star, or *slabozvezdo*. In contrast, many cultures believe that a leader or great person will have a bright star that shines clearly in the sky.

DRAGONS IN THE SKY

Another popular explanation for falling or shooting stars is that they are dragon- or serpent-like spirit creatures, blazing their way through the night sky, often wreaking havoc and destruction when they hit the earth.

In Belarus, if a star is seen falling fitfully rather than in a straight line, this is a strong indication that the star is actually a *zmej*. These creatures are often linked to evil magic; when a fireball is seen, it is said to be the *zmej* or devil carrying gold or silver for a witch or wizard, and that the star will fall over the location of the sorcerer's house. Likewise in Russia, it is said that a *zmej* or fireball is actually a flying witch or sorcerer. The Romanian *zmej* or *balauri* were malevolent creatures, waiting in the dark to leap on those people rash enough to be wandering alone at night, to disfigure or even kill them.

In Serbia, Bulgaria and Macedonia, the *zmej* is often known as *ala* or *hala*, which means 'snake' in Turkish. This creature can come down as a thick fog that stops corn from ripening and brings bad weather in general, such as great winds and storms. They live in caves out of the way of humankind when they can, guarding their treasure jealously. At the end of their lives, they become so large and filled with power that they cannot be contained on earth any longer; they leave altogether, and can be seen as shooting stars in the sky as they fly.

In Russia, the *zmej* or *zmey* as they are also known there, targets women who either pine too heavily or for too long for missing men-folk, or those that are dead.

The *zmey* appears in the likeness of the missing man to the woman (though no one but her can see it), and is said to have sexual intercourse with her. Malevolent meteor spirits in the form of serpents were recognized by several groups in the Northern Territory of Australia. They hunted for the souls of those who were ill or dying.

Such dragon spirits associated with meteors aren't always seen as malevolent, however. In Belarus, there is the *khut*, a household spirit that brings good fortune and wealth to a family. Likewise in Lithuania, the *aitvaras*, another meteor dragon, brings good fortune and wealth to the household it patronizes.

PART TWO
SUMPTUOUS SKIES

STALLIONS
OF THE SKIES:
Pegasus and Other
Soaring Steeds

Myth and fable abound with tales of winged horses, sweeping majestically through the skies, often taking their riders on glorious and perilous adventures to far-off lands where anything can – and quite often does – happen.

Without a doubt, one of the most famous and well-known winged horses is Pegasus of Greek mythology. Linked with the adventures of more than one Greek hero, this divine steed was a brilliant white, with large, resplendent wings that unfurled to an enormous width.

There are several different variations of the birth of Pegasus. In one account, the winged horse sprung forth from the spray of blood created when Perseus lopped off the head of the Gorgon Medusa. In some versions, Medusa was actually portrayed as a mare; Pegasus was foaled after her decapitation. In another, Pegasus came to be when Medusa's blood and pain mixed with sea foam, and is said to have been fathered by the sea god, Poseidon, who was also the god of horses.

According to one myth, in Lycia, a terrible, fire-breathing monster known as Chimera was causing great terror and destruction across the land. The king despaired of finding a hero who could slay the creature, when the hero Bellerophon arrived at the palace with letters of introduction from Proetos, the king's son-in-law. Those letters were a double-edged sword, however, as they also asked the king to slay Bellerophon, due to the fact Proetos felt his wife was giving the hero too much attention. The wily king quickly saw a solution: send Bellerophon to face the unstoppable monster.

As the king had hoped, Bellerophon accepted the impossible task. He took the advice of a soothsayer, who counselled him to find and master Pegasus, a great winged horse, and that he should start by spending a night in the Temple of Athena. Bellerophon did as he was instructed and, while he slept, the goddess came to him with a golden bridle. It was not just a dream, however: the bridle was in his hand when he awoke.

From there, Bellerophon went on to find Pegasus. He finally located the horse drinking from a stream; upon seeing the bridle, Pegasus allowed Bellerophon to mount him, before flying off into the air. They found the Chimera and Bellerophon defeated the terrible creature, bringing an end to its reign of terror. After that, Bellerophon went on to successfully complete many more trials with his faithful steed, and finally the king gave his daughter as his wife.

Pride comes before a fall, however, and fall Bellerophon did; when he attempted to fly high enough to enter heaven, where only the gods could dwell, Zeus punished his presumption by sending a gadfly to sting Pegasus. The startled stallion threw his rider, and Bellerophon fell to earth, where he lived out the rest of his days, lame and blind. After the fall of Bellerophon, Pegasus was taken up to Olympus where he lived in Zeus's stables, carrying thunderbolts for the god. He served Zeus so faithfully, that after a time he was rewarded by being turned into a constellation and placed among the stars. Pegasus can be seen today from the northern hemisphere from late summer throughout autumn, and in the southern hemisphere in late winter and into spring.

It was said that Pegasus had a power that meant wherever he stamped his hooves, a fresh water spring would flow from that spot. The most famous occasion of this was the creation of the Hippocrene – meaning 'horse spring' – fountain. On Mount Helicon, during a contest with the daughters of Pierus, the Muses played such beautiful music and sang so enchantingly that the earth and heavens themselves stilled: the mountain rose upwards, ascending towards where the gods lived. As with Bellepheron, such presumption could not be left unchecked: Poseidon, angered that the mountain moved without his say-so, sent Pegasus to the summit, where the great horse stamped his hooves to stop the mountain in its tracks. Water gushed forth from the spot, becoming the sacred fountain of Hippocrene.

Another snow-white winged horse is the Hindu Uchchaihshravas. This sacred steed was sometimes said to be the *vahana* – vehicle – of the king of the gods, Indra, and was, like Pegasus, pure white.

Indra is not the only god that Uchchaihshravas is associated with. In the *Bhagavad Gita*, he is identified with Krishna, when this god likens himself to Uchchaihshravas among horses, i.e., that Uchchaihshravas is king of the horses. In the *Vishnu Purana*, Uchchaihshravas is also named as king of the horses. Uchchaihshravas was also said to have been taken by Bali, king of the demons, who used the horse for many nefarious purposes.

How did Uchchaihshravas come into existence? According to the *Mahabharata*, Uchchaihshravas was created during the Samudra Manthana – the churning of the milk ocean – which also led to the appearance of several other great treasures, including the elixir of life, known as the *amrita*.

Uchchaihshravas was the focus of a bet between Vinata and Kadru, the wives of Kashyapa, over the colour of the horse's tail. The stakes were high: whoever lost the bet was to become the servant of the winner. Vinata bet that the tail was white, while Kadru chose black. Leaving nothing to chance, Kadru cheated; she instructed her serpent sons to cover Uchchaihshravas's tail, making it appear black as she had predicted, thus securing her victory.

According to the traditional tales of several Turkic-speaking nations, the Tulpar is another winged horse, known for its great speed. It is thought that this fantastical beast came about through the amalgamation of horses and birds of prey, used together for hunting in Central Asia. They were merged into one in the popular imagination, creating the mythical beast known as the Tulpar.

The most well-known tale involving the Tulpar involves the creation of the *morin khuur*, the Mongolian horse-headed fiddle. A sheep herder named Namjil is given a winged horse, magical and special, that went by the name of Jonon Har – Black Jonon. Busy with his master's sheep by day, come night time it was a very different story, as Namjil would mount his magical steed and fly to a far-off land to meet with the love of his life. Namjil's happiness however was destined to be jeopardized as one woman, overcome with jealousy, plotted his downfall, and employed someone to cut off Jonon Har's wings. Finding his beloved steed dead, the distraught herder created the fiddle from the horse's bones and skin, and used it to play songs about his lost friend for all to hear.

The Tulpar also features in the national emblem of Kazakhstan. Officially adopted in 1992, the emblem is circular in shape, with a *shanyrak* – an arched, cross-shaped top of a yurt – on a blue background. Sun rays or supports radiate from this, and on either side of the yurt is a Tulpar. According to the official website of the President of the Republic of Kazakhstan, the Tulpars represent bravery and the wings the dream of a nation that is prosperous and strong. The wings are also marked like sheaves of corn, representing the 'labour of the people of Kazakhstan and material welfare of the country'. Although the Tulpar could fly, the wings of a Tulpar were actually sometimes linked to the speed of the horse, not flight itself.

Another winged horse is the Qianlima, found in the Chinese classics, known throughout several countries of East Asia. Variously also known as Chollima and Cheollima, its name translates to 'thousand-li horse', referring to the fact it is said to be able to travel this distance – approximately 400km (250 miles) – in the space of one day. Also from Chinese folklore is Tianma, or 'heavenly horse'. This horse was sometimes depicted with dragon scales, and some sources say that it was able to sweat blood.

THE FLYING WAX
HORSE

In this tale from Sri Lanka, there was a king in a land far, far away. The king had a son and, wanting to know what the future held for him, he had the prince's horoscope drawn up. Once it was completed, the Brahmanas informed the king that when the prince reached adulthood, he would go away from his homeland. The king was not happy with this prospect, and as a result kept the prince guarded at all times. He even went so far as to have a special room prepared for him, on the highest floor of the palace, in order to keep him as safe and secure as possible.

When the prince was older, he spotted a winged horse made of wax for sale in the marketplace one day when he was out for entertainment. The prince begged his father for it and the king agreed, purchasing the horse for his son. This horse, however, was no ordinary toy; its wings were not for show, and the horse could actually fly. The prince was the only one to know this fact, and he kept his secret from everyone around him. No more was the prince confined to his home town; he used the horse to leave the palace and fly away to explore the realm beyond.

Alas for his father! One day, the prince left his country altogether, fulfilling the prophecy that had been made all those years before. As he flew, the prince came to the house of an old woman, who made garlands of flowers for the king of this kingdom. Concealing his flying horse in a tree, the prince went into the house, and there the woman told him all about the palace and the royal family who lived there. He learned that the princess, the king's daughter, had rooms on the top floor of the palace, and decided to go and see her and her home. The prince flew there at night and, while the princess was asleep, he saw the feasts that were

set out for her. Unable to resist, the prince helped himself, eating what he wished for several nights in a row without detection.

All was well until the princess noticed at last that food was going missing. She hatched a plan to stay awake to catch the person that was helping themselves to her victuals. The plan worked; catching the prince eating her food she accosted him at sword-point and demanded to know who he was.

The prince told her his name and where he had come from, along with the fact he was a prince. Despite this shaky start, the two took a liking to each other, and continued to meet: perhaps inevitably for such a tale, the prince and princess fell in love.

All would have perhaps been well, and their secret would have continued, if not for a strange habit of the princess's father. This king would weigh his daughter every morning, and noticed after a time that her weight was increasing. It was not long before the truth was revealed: the princess was with child.

Furious, the king suspected his minister of being the father, and immediately ordered that the man be killed. The poor man could do nothing about his fate, and his downcast demeanour did not go unnoticed. The other princesses of the palace noticed his plight, and when he revealed the cause of his despondence, they decided to save the poor man. They determined to prove that he was innocent and reveal the true identity of the man who had really been visiting their sister. The young women had an idea, and laced the scented water boat by the pool at the palace gateway with poison, knowing that the visitor would bathe there before meeting the princess, and thus his identity would be revealed.

Happily oblivious to such plotting, the prince came as usual to visit his love. He entered the bathing boat none the wiser, until the poison in the water burned his skin. In agony, the prince leapt out, before jumping into the pool in an attempt to soothe it. Alas, the pool was guarded by royal guards, and the prince was captured and taken before the king. The minister was set free, but the prince now found himself with a death sentence.

What was he to do? As he was being taken to the place of execution, the wily prince told his guards that something special that belonged to him was hidden outside the palace. He told them he would give it to them, if only they would let him go and fetch it.

Swayed by greed at the thought of what precious item the prince might have concealed, the guards agreed. The prince hurried to the tree where he had left his horse; quick as a flash, he climbed onto its back and flew away. He did not abandon his lover, however; that night he returned to the palace, taking the princess away with him.

As they flew, they passed over a thick forest. The princess could go no further: it was time for her child to come. They landed in the forest, and the prince settled his love safely before hurrying away on his horse to the nearby village for aid.

The prince left the horse outside a shop while he went into the one next door. As he was conducting his business, disaster struck: a fire broke out all of a sudden, and the wax horse was melted before he could do anything to save it. Not only had the prince lost his horse but, even worse, he could not find his way back to the forest and his love who was, perhaps even at that very moment, giving birth to their child. There was nothing he could do.

The princess, for her part, waited and waited for him to return, and in the meantime her baby, a boy, was born. The poor young woman, thinking her lover had abandoned her on purpose, eventually left the forest. She left the baby there too, unable to bear the thought of raising the child of such a selfish, heartless prince. She went to a nearby village, making her home there.

As luck would have it, the king, her father, rode through the very same forest. He found the child, alone and unprotected, and took him to the palace, where he raised him as one of his family, never suspecting for one moment that it was actually his own grandson all along.

Time passed, and the baby grew to be a fine prince. One day, he was travelling through the village where, unknown to him, his mother lived. She was with a group of local girls and, not knowing her true identity, he decided he wanted to propose marriage to her. On three occasions he tried to ask for her hand, and on all three a bad omen occurred to prevent him from doing so.

At the first attempt, his horse trampled some baby chickens. The mother hen angrily shouted at him: 'As it is insufficient that this one is going to take his mother in marriage, he killed my few young ones.'

Perplexed, he returned to the palace.

The next day he tried again, but this time his horse trampled a young goat. It too died, and the mother goat responded in the same way that the hen had. The prince then tried again one more time, but another similarly bad omen occurred, meaning he could not propose as he intended.

There was worse to come. The prince learned from the girls that he was unlikely to be able to marry anyone, due to his having been abandoned in the forest as a baby. No one knew who his parents were, so no one would give their daughter in marriage to him. Friends had also taunted him when younger for being illegitimate, and now it all made sense.

With all of this combined, the prince's suspicions were aroused, and he asked the king who he truly was. When faced with the question, the king told him all that he knew of his life and origins. The prince went back to the village to see the girls once more. He asked the princess about herself, and she told him her story. The prince realized then that she was actually his mother and, with this knowledge and knowing at last his true identity, the prince wasted no time in finding his own father, and they were happily reunited. He also brought his mother and father together again after so many years. The old king made the young prince the next in line for the throne, the young prince duly married a princess and they all lived together, happily ever after.

BIRDS OF MYTH AND LEGEND

Birds, those natural denizens of the sky, are frequently featured in many myths and legends, and they have come to stand as both symbols and portents in familiar and not so familiar tales. From the self-regenerating Phoenix to Odin's ravens, here are some of the most wonderful and revered birds from myth and legend.

Caladrius

The Caladrius is a bird found in Roman mythology, purported to have both prophetic and healing powers. This wondrous bird would be brought to the sickroom: if the bird turned its head away from the sufferer, then this was bad news and meant they would surely die; but if the Caladrius looked into the person's face then all would be well, they would recover and live. The Caladrius was said to actively aid in the recovery of the sick; it would absorb their sickness and then fly upwards to the sun, where the illness would be burned up and removed from both the sick person and the bird itself before it returned to earth.

Dung from the Caladrius was also believed to have restorative properties and to cure people of blindness. There was one catch, however: the dung had to be rubbed into the eyes of the afflicted person. This was sometimes commuted to having dung rubbed on the thigh bone, which may have been in order to make the practice less distasteful, or due to a confusion or mistranslation between *fimus* ('dung') and *femur* ('thigh bone'). Pliny the Elder named the bird *icterus* due to its yellowish colour, and said it was skilled at curing jaundice.

In medieval bestiaries, the bird was frequently used as an allegory for Christ, both in turning his face away from sinners who refused to repent and also due to the pure whiteness of the bird as represented in the volumes. This link is further cemented in the idea of the bird taking on people's sickness, representing Christ's saving of humankind.

The appearance of the Caladrius varies between sources. In medieval bestiaries the bird was often represented as either dove- or seagull-like in appearance, and was pure white. Mentioned in histories of Alexander the Great from the same period, the bird was shown with tan or yellow feathers and, in general in non-religious texts, the Caladrius was shown in varying colours. Other depictions

of the Caladrius include a sculpture from the 12th century in St Mary's Church, Alne, near York, and a 13th-century stained-glass window in the cathedral of Saint-Jean-Baptiste, Lyon, France.

The origins of the Caladrius are unknown and disputed; some believe it may have been based on a real bird, and potential contenders include the heron, dove, skylark or wagtail. Aristotle and other early Greek writers described a bird known as the charadrius; this creature was a water bird, or a bird that lived in a cave, and it is possible the Caladrius was developed from this bird.

Interest in the Caladrius seems to have died out by the 15th century, but curiosity about this mythical bird has seen a resurgence in recent years, and it is used in several health-related logos and symbols, such as that of the Isle of Wight Health Associates Cricket Club and the coat of arms for the Medical University of Southern Africa.

Huginn and Muninn

The name of Odin, king of the Norse gods, is a familiar one to many from myth and legend and, more recently, the highly popular Marvel movie franchise. How many know the details, however, of his two faithful feathered companions?

In Norse mythology, Huginn (meaning 'thought' in Old Norse) and Muninn (meaning 'memory' or 'mind') were two ravens, one perching on each of Odin's shoulders. The god would send them off each day with the dawn, and they would spend their hours flying across Midgard – earth – before returning to him in the evening. During their flight covering the whole span of the earth, these ravens would hear of everything that was happening, and report back to their master who had, according to some sources, given them the power of speech. In this way, Odin was greatly knowledgeable of all that went on across the earth, and learned a great deal from the two ravens.

It was said that Odin constantly worried that the ravens would not return to him at the end of the day, and was convinced that one day they would not come back. This fear was greater where Muninn was concerned, but it is not said exactly why. Some have interpreted this worry, and the meanings behind the names of the two ravens, to mean that the ravens symbolize a shamanic connection between Odin and the two birds, and that he was worried that he would not be able to return from a daily trance state. It has also been suggested that Odin was worried about his memory and losing control of his mind due to his advancing years. Others, however, point out that the names of the birds are likely to date to the 9th or 10th century CE at the earliest, whereas the birds themselves are believed to date from much earlier, thus weakening this argument. Supporting this, there is a 7th-century depiction of Odin on a helmet from Vendel, Sweden. On it, Odin is shown on horseback with two birds flying above him, believed to be an early depiction of his two ravens.

Some have made a connection between Odin and Merlin, the fabled magician of Arthurian legend, citing the fact that both were known to shape-shift and send forth their spirits. Odin was capable of transforming his shape – he changes into an eagle in order to steal the Mead of Poetry from the giants. There is also a theory that the Welsh Brân was once Odin, and came into being through translation or the corruption of the Germanic or Norse for raven.

Another link between ravens and Odin is the Raven Banner – a flag that was flown by several Viking chieftains and rulers in Scandinavia between the 9th and 11th centuries. With a rough triangular shape, the outside edge was rounded with tassels on it. Some believe that the raven depicted symbolizes Odin, with the purpose of terrifying the enemy.

Ravens are common throughout Norse mythology and belief, and have a strong connection to war and death, frequenting battlefields and being attracted to carrion there. Odin is likewise linked to death and battle, as he receives those who have died in battle when they reached Valhalla.

Firebird

The Firebird is perhaps the most iconic and well-known bird from Slavic folklore and fairy tales. In appearance, the bird was described as having bright, crystal-like eyes, and it glowed as if on fire; in some cases, it was actually said to burn. The Firebird's plumage is resplendent in shades of reds, yellows and oranges, a dazzling display that captivates all who see or hear of it. The feathers of a Firebird are said to remain glowing even when they have come loose.

There are many versions of the Firebird story due to the fact that such tales were originally conveyed in oral form. There are common themes throughout the tales of this elusive bird; it is often the treasured prize in a quest by a hero, who sets off to find the bird either after finding one of its tail feathers or being tasked with finding it by an authority figure, such as a father or the king or the tsar himself. The first written recorded version of the firebird tale was from the mid-19th century, *The Firebird, the Horse of Power and the Princess Vasilisa*. Tales of the Firebird were obviously in existence much earlier, however.

The themes of hunting a difficult treasure, or being on an arduous quest or journey, are also common themes associated with the bird. The Firebird was known for stealing apples from the garden of the tsar; in some versions of the tale, events revolve around attempts to stop the bird, with the tsar charging his sons with solving the problem. In another tale, a terrible magician is holding 13 beautiful princesses captive in his castle; the young Ivan discovers this when he captures the Firebird and sets it free, and is given a feather in reward for granting its freedom. Ivan falls in love with the fairest of the princesses, and ultimately defeats and kills the magician with the aid of the protection of the magical feather.

The Firebird is a mixed blessing; it is seen as a positive force, a treasure, a gift, but this can also turn and leave the quester wishing they had never come across the bird or its feathers. For it can also stand as a symbol of misfortune, peril and ultimate doom.

In more recent times, the Firebird has erroneously come to be conflated in some cases with the legendary Phoenix, but the two birds are very distinct creatures. Although they share some similarities, the big difference is the Phoenix's self-combustion and resurrection every 500 years.

Ziz

The Ziz is a mythical bird from Jewish tradition. This giant creature was a sight to behold – when it spread its wings, it was said that it blocked out the very light from the sun, causing a solar eclipse. Standing on the floor of the deepest ocean, the water barely reached its ankles, with its head reaching up to touch the sky.

In appearance, the Ziz has been likened to the legendary griffin. It has the head and wings of a bird, with the back legs of a lion. The Ziz is often linked with the other great beasts, Leviathan who rules the sea and Behemoth who rules the land, with Ziz named as the ruler of the sky, the third creature in a mythological triumvirate.

According to a tale in the Babylonian Talmud, a group of travellers in a boat caught sight of the Ziz standing in the water close by. They assumed the water was shallow as it was only reaching as far as the bird's ankles. Tragedy was averted when a voice from above called to them, warning them that the water was not as it appeared; a carpenter's axe had been dropped into that very spot seven years ago, and the axe had not yet reached the bottom!

Another tale pays further testament to the great size of this bird. Once an egg belonging to the Ziz fell from its nest, smashing as it hit the ground. The contents of the egg were so great that it destroyed 300 cedar trees and flooded 16 cities.

Fenghuang

The Fenghuang is a mythological bird found in Chinese, Japanese and Vietnamese cultures. First depicted in art around 8,000 years ago, the Fenghuang has a long history, as splendid and varied as the bird itself.

The Fenghuang is said to be six chi – 2.7m (9ft) – tall. In appearance, descriptions of the bird vary: originally, the Fenghuang was said to be a composite of several creatures, with the head of a cock, a swallow's beak, the neck of a snake, a tortoise's back and the tail of a fish. In more recent times, a common description includes the head of a golden pheasant, a parrot's beak, crane's legs, the body of a mandarin duck and wings of a swallow. Colour-wise, there are also variations: the bird is variously described as black, white, red, yellow and green.

The different parts of a Fenghuang are each said to stand for a different aspect of space: the feet represent the earth, the head the sky, the back the moon, wings the wind, tail the planets and eyes the sun. It is generally accepted that the Fenghuang has actually shifted gender over time, moving from yang (male) to yin (female). In modern times, the female Fenghuang is a familiar sight, paired with the male Chinese dragon.

Misleadingly referred to at times as the Chinese Phoenix, the Fenghuang is one of China's most famous mythical birds. The links with the Phoenix are misleading, as the two birds are actually entirely different and have different origins. The connection between the two birds is believed to have arisen due to 19th-century textual translations from Chinese to English, and highlights the difficulties and impact of cultural assumptions and misinterpretation: the Fenghuang is culturally specific to Chinese culture and cannot be cleanly translated into a Western cultural experience, so the word 'phoenix' was used frequently to be more easily understood by Western readers. This conflation or interchangeability of the two birds is still seen today: in the 2020 Disney film *Mulan*, a Phoenix represents the Fenghuang.

The Fenghuang was said to govern one of the four quadrants of the heavens, one of four sacred creatures to do so; Fenghuang ruled the southern quadrant. It made its home in the K'unlan Mountains, living there within wu tung trees. The song of the Fenghuang was believed to be such a magical sound that its song was the inspiration for the Chinese harmonic scale itself.

A peaceful creature, the Fenghuang was known for eating bamboo seeds. Associated with summer, the sun and fire, from the Zhou dynasty onwards it was also linked with harmony, peace and political prosperity. Seeing a Fenghuang is said to be a sign of good luck, a good omen for times ahead. The bird was also believed to only appear during times of prosperity and during peaceful, well-governed reigns. No one knows for certain where the Fenghuang myth originated, but it has been suggested that it might actually be based on a real creature, such as an ostrich-like prehistoric bird.

One popular legend relating to the Fenghuang is that it appeared before the death of the Yellow Emperor, Huangdi, in the 27th century BCE. The bird is also said to have appeared at the grave of Emperor Hongwu, founder of the Ming Dynasty.

Today, the Fenghuang is a familiar decorative choice for religious ceremonies and weddings, and is also popular in jewellery design.

THE FIREBIRD

Long ago in Russia there was a girl called Marushka. This young orphan was a good-natured girl, gentle, modest and quiet, and none could fault her. She was also wonderfully skilled with a needle, and there was no one who could do such fine embroidery as Marushka. She made many beautiful items for people, from shirts to sashes and much in between, using silks and beautiful beads made of glass. Whatever she was paid for her work she was content, and never complained, even when it was worth much more than she was offered.

Many merchants from both near and far-off lands heard of Marushka's talent, and many came to witness it for themselves. Amazed, they gazed on in awe, never having seen work so beautiful in their lives. Captivated, each visitor asked Marushka to leave her life to live with them, and each offered her things they believed she could never refuse. But the girl surprised them all, telling each simply that she was content where she was. She would not leave her village, she told them, and riches held no interest for her. She would continue to sell her work to those who wished to own it, but she would remain where she was.

The rejected merchants were greatly disappointed, but there was nothing they could do, and each went on their way, telling those they met as they went on their travels about the girl with the unforgettable embroidery. In this way, word of Marushka eventually reached a wicked, wicked sorcerer, none other than the terrible Kaschei the Immortal himself. This terrible man immediately flew into a great rage, angry beyond measure that there dared to exist such beauty in the world that he had not personally witnessed.

Kaschei transformed his appearance into a young, handsome man, and flew his way across all manner of terrain to the cottage

where the unsuspecting girl lived. Knocking at the door, he waited patiently, politely bowing low when she opened it to him. He asked then to see her needlework, and Marushka duly laid out everything she had: handkerchiefs, towels, shirts and veils – each item more beautiful and impressive than the last. She told the sorcerer that he could take whatever he wished, and if he had no money with him then, it was no issue: he could pay her later when he was able to. If there was nothing that appealed to him, Marushka continued, he had only to tell her, and she would make something that fit with his requirements.

Rather than being impressed by her kindness and the quality of her work, Kaschei grew still angrier. For all the fine things he owned, how was it that this simple girl from the countryside could make things so much finer than anything he possessed? He was the greatest of sorcerers and had whatever he wanted, but he just could not compete with Marushka's splendid work.

Determined to have what he wanted at all costs, the sorcerer applied all his wit and cunning to the situation. He told Marushka that if she came with him, he would make her a queen, filling her head with all manner of wonderful and precious things that she would have if only she would leave her home and go with him. Gold plates for her meals, a bejewelled palace, and an orchard with golden apples and beautiful birds singing the sweetest songs known to humankind were among the things he offered her, certain that Marushka would not be able to say no.

The sorcerer was wrong, and Marushka rejected him, not tempted for one moment by all that he dangled before her. She had no need of such riches or the things he offered: for right where she was she had the woods and fields where she had lived since she was born, and there was nothing sweeter to Marushka. Not only that, but she would never willingly abandon the graves of her parents, or leave the people who found such joy in her work. No, Marushka told him firmly, she would not embroider for one man alone, whatever riches he offered her.

The furious Kaschei could not believe anyone could defy him so. In a rage he shouted that Marushka would be a maiden no longer, but instead would be a bird for evermore. No sooner had the words left his lips than a Firebird appeared where moments before Marushka had been standing. In turn, the sorcerer transformed himself into a giant black falcon. In this form, he soared high into the sky before swooping down to capture the Firebird, strong, cruel talons gripping her tight.

But Marushka would not be beaten, and would not leave her homeland without leaving some long-enduring memory of herself there among the people and places that she so loved. As she rose she shed her brilliant feathers, and they fell, one by one, down to the ground below. Landing in the forests and the meadows, there they lay, a rainbow reminder for all to see of Marushka and her beautiful embroidery.

COME RAIN OR SHINE:
Weather Lore and Superstitions

The state of the weather has always been a vitally necessary preoccupation of humankind, the effects of fair weather or foul affecting our daily lives and, quite literally in some cases, determining our very survival. Unsurprisingly, therefore, there is an equally long history of belief that certain signs in the natural world can predict what weather will follow, with a vast number of superstitions, sayings and adages growing from these signs and predictions. Passed down through the spoken and printed word, some hold scientific backing, others decidedly less so, but regardless, many remain deeply entrenched in our collective psyche today. Some beliefs and sayings prove to be almost universal, while others are relevant only to the particular weather and climate conditions of specific countries. The wide glut of weather-related superstitions and sayings in existence are far too numerous to cover in their entirety, but here is a tour through some of the most popular – and some less well-known – weather sayings and superstitions from around the world.

For obvious reasons, the appearance of the sky features heavily in weather lore. One very familiar idea is that if the sky and clouds are tinged red at specific times of the day this is a sign of either rain or fair weather to come, as in the ever popular:

Red sky at night, shepherd's delight,
red sky in the morning, shepherd's warning.

The belief that red sky has great significance has a long provenance; in the Bible in Matthew, 16:3, Jesus says: 'When it is evening, ye say, fair weather: for heaven is red. And in the morning foul weather today: for the heaven is red and lowering.' Theophrastus recorded beliefs about the importance of red skies in the 3rd century BCE, stating that a red sky before dawn would mean rain either on that day, or within three days. A red sky at sunset would also potentially mean rain within three days, though this was less concrete.

'Evening red and morning grey are sure signs of a fine day. Evening grey and morning red, put on your hat or you'll wet your head,' is another instance of red skies being cited. According to another saying, 'Red morning skies fill the well, red evening skies dry it,' meaning red sky in the morning heralded rain. According to some, a red morning sky on New Year's Day was said to mean thunderstorms and general bad happenings would occur.

What causes these red skies in the first place? Scientifically, red skies at sunset are caused by blue light being scattered when dust and small particles are caught in the atmosphere by high pressure, and often does indicate fair weather the following day, as it is a sign of high pressure moving in from the west. According to Germanic mythology, a red sky in the evening was caused by a giant doing battle with the spirits of light. Another explanation was that the Virgin Mary was making cakes for Christmas.

The shape or form of the clouds is also considered important when it comes to predicting the weather. One widely held belief is that clouds looking like the scales of a mackerel predict certain weather, for instance in the saying: 'Mackerel sky, mackerel sky, never long wet, never long dry'. Another similar idea was that 'Mackerel sky and mares' tails, make lofty ships carry low sails,' warning that a storm and high winds were on the way and that the sails should therefore be lowered.

Don't let us forget the significance of the sun, moon and other celestial bodies when it comes to being harbingers of weather to come. Black spots on either the sun or moon were said to be a sign of rain, but if the spots were red, then wind was due instead. A halo around the moon or sun is also a sign that wind is due. If there is a break in either halo, take note of its position: the wind will come from that direction.

Another common method of predicting the weather is the less scientific yet equally popular belief that weather at certain times of the year can predict weather at a different time of year, with one being dependent upon the other. Such seemingly spurious ideas actually shed an important light on the impact weather can have on humankind as a whole: a vast number of such correlating predictions involve predicting whether the coming winter will be harsh or mild, reflecting the grim fact that at many times this could very often be the difference between survival or otherwise.

One belief with a long heritage is that of the predictive abilities of the weather in early February. It is said that the weather at this time can predict how much longer the winter will continue. In many countries, including England, Germany, France and Scotland, it is believed that the weather on Candlemas Day, 2 February, will predict how long winter will continue. One popular saying is: 'Candlemas Day be fair and bright, winter will take a second flight', meaning that if the weather is fine on Candlemas, then winter will come back for a final harsh spell before finally giving way to spring.

In both England and Germany there has been a belief since at least the 16th century that the day upon which Christmas Day falls will determine how the winter weather pans out. For example, if Christmas Day falls on a Thursday, the winter will be a windy one, whereas Christmas Day on a Friday means a winter of hard frosts and snow. In Sweden, weather on 30 November, St Andrew's Day, is also an important predictor, as in '*Anders slaskar, julen braskar*', i.e., 'slushy Anders, frozen Christmas'. Another belief is, 'If ice in November can bear a duck, the rest of the winter'll be slush and muck'.

According to the Hispanic *cabañuelas*, the first 12, 18 or 24 days of January or August will predict what the weather will be like for the rest of the year.

It is not only in the skies that we look for these patterns of cause and effect: we have extended our horizons to the behaviour of birds, animals and even insects, finding correlations between their actions and the weather. Animals are said to be particularly sensitive to changes in the air or temperature, and are believed to be able to feel approaching weather before we do. Whatever the truth of this, they are frequently credited with the power to unwittingly forecast the weather, a belief reflected in the wide abundance of sayings linking the two.

If an ass has its ears forwards and downwards, then rain should be expected, and the same if the animal is rubbing against the walls or braying more often than usual, as reflected in the saying from Tyrol, modern-day Austria, that *'Wenn oft die Esel schreien kommt schlechtes Wetter'*. In Bergamo, Italy, it was said that when asses pricked their ears or sneezed, a change in the weather was due, and rain was on the way.

Cattle are also believed to know when rain is coming: a popular belief is that when they are lying down – sometimes specifically in the morning – rain will follow soon. In a proverb from Ariège, France, if cattle huddled together, then rain was due. This could also be true if cattle sniffed the air, lay on their right side, or licked their front feet. A Venetian proverb states that: *'Co la vaca tien su'l muso, Bruto tempo salta suso'*. Meaning that if a cow sniffs the air with its nostrils turned upwards, then bad weather is to be expected. The same is true if they lie on their right side or lick their forefeet.

According to Bretagne lore, *'Chien qui se roule annonce du vent: s'il mange de l'herbe, il pleuvra'* – if a dog is rolling on the ground, then a strong wind is said to follow; if the dog lies on its right side, there will be fair weather; but if it eats grass, rain will come. A saying from Germany holds that if dogs bark at the moon, then it's time to wrap up warm, as a severe cold snap will soon be on the way.

Hedgehogs might seem a surprising candidate for weather prediction, but according to various beliefs they are said to have foreknowledge of when windy weather is due. The animal is said to make two holes underground, one towards the north, and the other towards the south. If the hedgehog blocks one of the holes, then that is the direction the wind will be coming from. Be especially wary if the hedgehog blocks both holes – violent wind is not far away. It is also said that whichever way the hedgehog builds its nest, the wind will blow from the opposite direction.

Snails are believed to forecast rain: if there are lots out in the evening, then it will be a rainy night. There is some basis in fact: snails do come out when it rains, as do slugs. An intriguing snippet from Georgia in the *American Meteorological Journal* refers to a certain type of snail that changed colour when rain was due, but no further information was available on this intriguing occurrence.

Frogs were commonly believed in German-speaking areas of the world to be able to predict the weather. If green frogs chirruped in a tree, or if toads were taking a bath or making a lot of noise, then rain should be expected. If a tree frog is croaking on its own in the early dawn, then a storm is coming.

Out at sea, dolphins diving and then reappearing several times when near land are said to predict rain or a storm, as does the appearance of a large number of jellyfish.

How do birds fare against their fellow creatures in the prediction department? A common belief found in South Africa, Ukraine and other areas regarding swallows is that when they fly low then rain is due. Another belief is that when cranes take flight and don't return, then good weather is ahead. If cranes appear early in the autumn, however, then winter will be harsh, while cranes soaring quietly is another reason to expect good weather – but if they are loud, then a storm is due. Corvids are also said to be handy barometers: crows, diving or hovering over water, or a raven making a whirring sound and shaking its wings, or flying high and screaming, means rain. Likewise, if a lone raven makes three croaks, then repeats this over and over, rain is due. If a crow caws three times at the break of dawn, it is a good sign: fair weather is coming. Generally, when non-water birds bathe, then rain or a storm should be expected. In Australia, when kookaburras call in winter, it is said that rain will fall, as is the case when black cockatoos fly and call.

A common belief from the coastal areas of many countries is that gulls will head for land when bad weather is due. This is reflected in such sayings as: 'Seagull, seagull, sit on the sand, it's never good weather when you're on the land.' In some areas of the United States, this is believed to the extent that some people will leave a beach when they see gulls leaving in large numbers.

The cuckoo – also called the rain cow in the USA – is one of the best-known signs of rain in the animal kingdom, a belief found in many countries across the world. This is a long-held idea: according to Hesiod, when one was heard, three days of rain were to be expected. In South Africa, the Burchell's coucal, a type of cuckoo also known as the 'rain bird', is also said to be heard when a storm is forming.

In a popular belief from the Cape Peninsula, South Africa, bad weather is expected in the afternoon if the bokmakierie calls before dawn and carries on for several hours. An AmaXhosa belief states that the bird's sound changes to a trill when rain is due. There is also rain due if the southern boubou calls while sitting under a bush.

And what of insects? If ants have an anthill in a hollow and are seen to carry their eggs to higher ground, it is said that there is rain to come. If the ants carry their eggs downwards, however, then fair weather is to be expected. In a belief from Australia, if ants travel in a straight line, then expect rain, but expect fine weather if they move in a more scattered form. Bees are said to 'never swarm before a storm', so if you see bees swarming then it is probably safe to venture out without your umbrella!

Humans themselves are also said to have some ability when it comes to predicting what weather lies ahead. This is often said to show itself in physical indications in the body: swelling feet, for instance, is said to mean that a southerly wind is due, potentially in some cases even a hurricane. Aching joints in general is often believed to mean bad weather is on the way.

Finally, signs can also be found in other, everyday items. Smoke falling from a chimney is said to mean a storm, as does a water-filled pot causing sparks when it is set on the fire. If a fire has embers looking like hailstones, then hail is to be expected. Fire or a lamp that cannot be lit despite repeated attempts is a sign of a storm, whereas a lot of ash means snow. A lamp burning quietly during a storm is a sign of good weather to come. Cobwebs dancing means wind is coming. In Iceland, if you leave a rake in the yard with the prongs up, beware: you might cause it to rain!

GROUNDHOG DAY

In the United States and Canada, 2 February is known as Groundhog Day, the day when the groundhog or woodchuck is said to come out of his den. If he sees his shadow, so the saying goes, the creature will return inside and stay there for another six weeks, meaning winter will last that much longer.

Groundhog Day celebrations are hugely popular in the northern USA and Canada and are celebrated in many towns and cities. A long line of weather-predicting groundhogs started in 1887 with a groundhog called Phil in Punxsutawney, Pennsylvania, and it has been declared that each successive 'Phil' is the only true weather-forecasting hog. Indeed, the largest Groundhog Day gathering is held in Punxsutawney each year, where as many as 40,000 gather to watch Phil as he emerges.

Over time however, many other towns across the USA have adopted their own special groundhogs, whose behaviour on 2 February is observed locally with great interest. Not everyone is as confident in the groundhog's predictive abilities, however: according to Oregon Zoo, it is actually hedgehogs that have the gift of forecasting the remainder of winter, and their own hog, FuFu, is the best of them all.

Where does this belief come from? The idea that the behaviour of a certain animal around the start of February could predict the outcome of the rest of winter dates back to at least Roman times. In Germany,

it was the behaviour of the badger on this day that was watched closely: Candlemas Day was Badger Day, Dachstag, and if the badger came out of its set and cast a shadow due to it being sunny, then it meant four more weeks of winter. This idea was transported to the USA where the groundhog was adopted instead.

Is there any truth in this belief? It might surprise some to read, but there is actually a grain of truth in the groundhog's actions. In February, male groundhogs do indeed come out of their burrows, but it is in search of a mate, not for any weather-predicting purpose. They then return until their hibernation ends in March and they emerge properly for the year.

Similarly, in Croatia and Serbia, either on Candlemas or on Sretenje, 15 February, it is said that the bear awakens from its winter sleep. If it sees or meets its own shadow, the bear will go back to sleep for another 40 days and winter will carry on. If it is cloudy, however, winter is going to end soon. In Ireland, seeing a hedgehog on St Brigid's Day, 1 February, was a sign of good weather ahead.

CHRISTENING THE APPLES:
WEATHER FORECASTING
WITH ST SWITHIN

Despite the blistering heatwaves of recent years and the urgent threat of climate change, gentle, warm summers are still on many a wish list; long, sunny days that mean fun days out with friends and family, healthy crops nourished by the sun's rays for a good harvest, and enough fair memories to tide us over the harsh cold winter to follow. While it is impossible to predict exactly what the weather may bring, having some sort of assurance that the days will be fine is always nice and, according to one particular piece of weather lore popular across Great Britain, we can have just that.

> *St Swithin's Day, if thou dost rain,*
> *For forty days it will remain.*
> *St Swithin's Day, if thou be fair,*
> *For forty days 'twill rain nae mair.*

Thus if St Swithin's Day – 15 July – dawns fair and dry, rejoice, because 40 days of sun and good weather lie ahead. If it is raining on that day, however, beware, for 40 days of rain are sure to follow.

How did such a superstition come about? According to legend, St Swithin, the 9th-century Bishop of Winchester, England, asked to be buried outside, where rain and the footfall of passers-by could land on his resting place. However, on 15 July 971, only a few years after his death, it was decided to move his remains to inside the cathedral instead, and a terrible storm is said to have broken out that lasted for 40 days, hence the association we have between the saint and the weather today.

Perhaps thankfully, the prediction is yet to come true: since records began in 1861, there has never been recorded a period of 40 consecutive days of either rain or sunshine following St Swithin's Day.

In another belief, if it rains on St Swithin's Day, it is said that he is baptizing and blessing the apples. Therefore it was not a good idea to pick apples before that date as they would not have been blessed yet.

St Swithin doesn't hold the monopoly when it comes to foretelling the fate of summer. In France, St Medard, commemorated on 8 June, is likewise considered important, with the saying, *'Quand il pleut a la St Médard, il pleut quarante jous plus tard'* – 'If it rains on St Medard's Day, it rains for 40 days more'.

It is said that this 5th-century reluctant future Bishop of Vermandois' association with rain came from the fact that, as a child, he was sheltered from the elements by a passing eagle. In later times, people prayed to him for rain if needed, or against bad weather if fine weather was wanted instead.

Medard is also known in England, in such sayings as, 'St Medard drops drop for 40 days,' or, 'On St Medard's Day it rains six weeks before or six weeks after.'

In France, the martyred twins St Gervase and St Protais (19 June) have similar predictions associated with them. St Godelieve's Day (6 July) is likewise important in Belgium. Rain is looked upon with horror on that day, as it means much more ahead. Across much of Europe, the weather on 27 June, the date commemorating the legend of the Seven Sleepers of Ephesus, is also said to forecast what weather lies ahead for summer. In Germany, the weather on Siebenschläfer Is watched with great care, as '*Das Wetter am Siebenschläfertag sieben Wochen bleiben mag*' – the weather on Seven Sleepers' Day may stay seven weeks.

RAISING UP A STORM:
Witches, Tempestarii
and Weather Magic

Weather: unpredictable, ungovernable and, in extreme cases, deadly; as we have already seen, humankind has, out of necessity, been fascinated by all things meteorological since our existence began. Whether through raging storms, terrible winds or earth-scorching droughts, across the globe we experience Mother Nature at her untameable finest. With the power to nourish life-giving crops or spoil a harvest and plunge a community into starvation, people, habitually at the mercy of her seeming whims, have approached the elements with both fear and awe, and observing and predicting the weather has understandably become an important preoccupation.

What, though, if there was a way to control these powerful elements? It would be the ultimate accomplishment: one who could control the weather could control life itself. Throughout history, across many cultures and continents, there have been those said to be able to do just that: to bring rain and raging storms and hail to destroy those who they dislike, and fine weather to suit their own nefarious purposes. The idea that there existed those who could control the weather has a long provenance, stretching back into antiquity, when it was said that powerful weather sorcerers, known as Tempestarii, could whip up storms at will.

Such beliefs prevailed through the centuries that followed. Writing in 815, Bishop Agobard of Lyons lamented that the belief that thunder and hailstorms were caused by men was widespread through all levels of society. Powerful 'storm makers' were said to raise the winds through their terrible incantations, bringing great

harm to crops and people. This belief went further still, much to the bishop's incredulous and scathing disbelief; it was believed that people from a region called Magonia flew in ships through the sky and paid a tribute to the storm makers, who then allowed them to take away the damaged crops and grain in the wake of their destruction. Agobard even related how four of these people – three men and one woman – had apparently been captured, bound in chains and nearly stoned, before common sense thankfully intervened. The entire lamentable situation was self-perpetuating, as there were people who in turn promised that they could protect crops against the storm raisers – charging, of course, for their services. People paid them tribute, to which Agobard particularly objected.

Many cultures have had individuals who are said to be able to influence the weather and call up storms and rain for good or ill, and there were several who were accused of (and in some cases admitted to) doing so. During the persecution of the Cathars in the 12th and 13th centuries, some confessed to asking devils to raise storms and other bad weather, and were therefore said to be responsible with the devil for destroying the crops of those they disliked. Off the coast of Brittany were said to live priestesses who controlled the tempests and winds.

During the period of the witch trials in continental Europe, belief in weather magic was rife, and the elements had become a dangerous weapon. Although previously only infrequently heard of, by 1570 accusations of negatively affecting the weather and using weather magic was common in trial accounts and printed texts. When accused, many people confessed, further fuelling the belief that witches could and did affect the weather, and reinforcing the perceived need for further persecution.

James VI of Scotland, I of England, was no stranger to the idea of weather magic. The 'Witch King', so called because of the dogged interest he took in witches at the start of his reign, believed he had first-hand experience of what witches could do with the weather. His future queen, Anne of Denmark, was unable to travel to Scotland as intended when, more than once, storms prevented her ship from setting off. James instead made his way to meet her, but on the couple's journey home they were beset with more terrible weather. The king was determined to make those he believed responsible pay, resulting in the North Berwick witch trials of the 1590s and the execution of dozens of suspected witches. James went on to write his famous text *Daemonologie*, in which he stated that witches 'can raise storms and tempests in the air either upon sea or land', further spreading this idea.

Isobel Gowdie, convicted of witchcraft in 1662, confessed that she and her fellow witches used their powers to raise winds. According to her confessions, 'When we raise the wind, we take a rag of cloth, and wet it in water; and we take a beetle [a wooden paddle or beater] and knock the rag on a stone, and we say thrice over: "I knock this rag upon this stane, To raise the wind, in the Devil's name; It shall not lie until I please again!"'

'When we would lay the wind, we dry the rag, and say (thrice over): "We lay the wind in the Devil's name, [It shall not] rise while we [or I] like to raise it again!"'

In England in 1645, Mary Lakeland, the only accused witch to face death at the stake in that country (though this punishment was for the supposed murder of her husband, not for witchcraft itself), was also accused of influencing the weather: she was said to have sunk the ship of a man who had slighted her granddaughter.

During the Vardø witch trials in Norway, a terrible storm took place where 40 men were drowned and many boats sunk. Under torture, Else Knutsdatter confessed that she and her coven of fellow witches had summoned the storm in December 1617. They had tied a fishing rope three times and spat on it. They then untied the rope to set the winds free to wreak their terrible damage. Else was burned at the stake.

Believing wholeheartedly in such a threat, people were fearful, and inevitably wanted to know how to counteract these terrible powers. Such beliefs were held throughout all levels of society: in a papal bull in the 15th century, Pope Innocent VIII acknowledged that those of both sexes were responsible for the blasting of others' crops. The authorities attempted at various points to control this perceived problem, with varying success. Legislation from the 6th and 7th centuries condemned the use of weather magic and the conjuring of storms, and the Church Council in Paris in 829 said that people doing so should be punished harshly. Similarly, punishment for the crime of storm making was penances of seven years, three of those on bread and water.

There were those who objected to the belief in weather magic itself: only God could control the weather, and it was blasphemous to say that anyone else could. But what if God was *allowing* witches and their evil companions to do so, in order to punish humankind for their sins? Debate raged over just what influence witches could have over the weather, with ideas changing and shifting over time, but generally, when acknowledged, controlling the weather was seen by the Christian Church as demonic, caused by demons and evil magic.

Naturally, people came up with their own ways of attempting to protect themselves from such powers, treading the fine line between holy actions and the magic that was being condemned. There were rituals that were permitted, however, and people were not left entirely helpless. It was believed that the ringing of consecrated church bells could chase away a thunderstorm, the evil spirits held responsible for thunder and lightning powerless against the might of the bells as they were rung out when the storm arrived. It was also common for Masses to be said to ensure good weather, and processions to counter bad harvests and weather. According to the *Malleus Maleficarum*, making the sign of the cross with leaves and consecrated flowers on Palm Sunday could protect against weather magic. The leaves would then be set in the fields with the crops to be protected, with the belief that the bad magic wouldn't be able to touch them because of it.

A way to stop a storm altogether involved three hailstones from the storm in question, and a series of incantations. These holy phrases were to be said as the hailstones were cast into a fire lit specifically for that purpose, and words of scripture and other holy words – including the Lord's Prayer, the Angelic Salutation, the Gospel of John and invoking the Holy Trinity – would bring the storm to an end as the sign of the cross was made in every direction. And if such measures didn't work? Then the storm was clearly of natural origins and not caused by a witch in the first place.

THE WESTRAY STORM WITCH

There are many times in folklore when fact and fiction blend together, creating the tales passed down through the ages. One such occasion is the legend of Janet Forsyth, the Storm Witch from Orkney, Scotland.

In 1629, Janet stood trial accused of witchcraft; among the charges against her were that she had caused illness to a woman, taken the fat from the cows' milk, cursed those who refused her food and drink, and bewitched a man into illness at sea, before – equally damningly – making him well again by washing him in saltwater. Janet was found guilty and sentenced to be strangled and then burned at the execution site in Clay Loan, Kirkwall, Orkney.

Despite this grim conclusion to Janet's life, legend and folklore has created another, happier ending for the woman now best known as the Westray Storm Witch.

According to the more palatable tale, in 1627, Janet had a dream that woke her in a terrible sweat, her heart pounding in terror. For in her nightmare, she had seen her lover, Benjamin Garrioch, drowned at sea, while she looked on, powerless to stop the tragedy.

As fate would have it, the day after, Ben Garrioch was due to go fishing with several local men. The day was fine, with no sign of bad weather, but on account of her dream, Janet pleaded with her love not to go. Garrioch brushed aside her concerns, and however much she pleaded with him to stay safely on dry land, Ben duly set off with the others. Oh, that he had listened! Out at sea a thick, roiling fog came from nowhere. It was too late for help, and none of the men returned home, lost at sea as Janet had predicted. Not only was she struck with the most terrible grief, but Janet was blamed for their deaths; she was a witch, people said, and had summoned the fog.

She was shunned, an outcast now, but Janet did not care. Heartbroken, she spurned the company of others, shutting herself away in her cottage. There Janet stayed and, slowly but surely, she became accused of being behind all bad weather, and whenever there was a storm it was Janet, they said, causing it along with all manner of other dreadful deeds.

One day, several years later, a struggling ship was spied offshore. The islanders, already thinking of what they could salvage from the wreckage, looked on, but Janet pleaded with them to help. None would agree, so Janet, not to be dissuaded, went alone. The howling wind and lashing rain did not abate, but Janet did not give up; rowing her small boat, she went out into the gale, getting close enough to the ship to lead it safely into the bay.

Far from being feted for her bravery, this altruistic act was Janet's downfall. For how could a single woman do battle against such a storm and emerge victorious? It was impossible: any other would have perished. There was only one answer: witchcraft.

On 11 November 1629, Janet was tried, found guilty and sentenced to death. Then, nothing short of a miracle occurred. For as her gaze roved over the watching, hungry crowd in the courtroom, she spied a painfully familiar face: Benjamin Garrioch, wearing the uniform of a naval man, alive against all odds. 'Save me, Ben!' she screamed at the top of her lungs, as guards dragged her away to the dungeon, Marwick's Hole, in St Magnus Cathedral, Kirkwall.

No one knows exactly what happened next. One thing is known for certain, however: the following morning, when they went to collect her for execution, Janet was nowhere to be seen, the dungeon empty. Where was she? Legend says that Ben Garrioch saved the day, sweeping in to rescue his sweetheart and taking her far away. It is said that they escaped together, perhaps to England, where they lived out their days together in perfect happiness.

CARRIED AWAY
BY THE WIND

According to one Polish tale, there was once a young man, poor and hard-working, who greatly angered a powerful magician. What he did to inspire such ire was not recorded, but the magician came one day to the hut where the young man lived and, going to the threshold, he stuck a sharp new knife underneath it. As he did so, the magician muttered a terrible spell, along with the desire that the man be swept up into the air by the wind. Not only that, the magician decreed that he was to remain there for seven long years.

The oblivious young man, with no inkling of what lay before him, made his way into the fields as usual to make hay. As he was working, a powerful wind rose up, blowing the hay this way and that across the fields. The man had no time to wonder at it, however, as he himself was caught up by the wind in that moment. He struggled and fought, and even tried to stop the inevitable by catching hold of trees and hedges as he went, but it was no good, and he was carried up, up, up and away.

He flew and flew, borne over the land like some sort of bird. The sun was starting to go down, and the tired and hungry man looked down to see his own village beneath him. Smoke was rising from the chimneys as the evening meal was being cooked, and he found he could almost touch them with his feet as he passed at one point. Surely someone would hear him? He screamed as loud as he could, but no one heard, no matter how hard and noisily he shouted and cried for help.

The poor man was carried thus for nearly three months. With nothing to eat or drink at all through that time he became so dried out that he was like a piece of wood. He was carried great distances, spinning and flying over great areas of the world that he had never seen before. But, as if to particularly torment him, he was forced to fly above his own village for much of the time, seeing everything he missed and held dear beneath him.

To add further to his torment, the man could see the very hut where the woman he was betrothed to lived. He watched, helpless, as she came and went, wanting nothing more than to throw his arms around her. He cast his arms out wide, trying to call her name, but he could get no closer, and his voice, dry and cracked now, could not reach her. No wonder then that she did not even look up; she had no idea of his presence.

At one moment, as he went by, the man saw a magician – the very one responsible for his predicament – standing in front of his own home. If the man hoped for mercy, then he was to be sadly disillusioned; the magician called up to him telling him that he would be held by the wind for the next seven years, condemned to look down on his own village and suffer constantly. He would not die, but might well wish for it.

The man cried down his sorrow and his apology, telling the magician that he had never meant to cause offence, and begged for mercy and pardon. The man suddenly found himself no longer spinning, held in the air by an invisible force, still under the magician's control. What, the magician asked, would the man give him if he were to let him down to earth once more?

'Anything!' the poor man replied instantly. He would give the magician whatever he asked for if only he could feel the earth beneath his feet again. Unfortunately for the man, the magician fixed on the one thing that he would find hardest to give up: the woman he loved and intended to marry.

The magician wanted her for his own wife.

How the man's heart went cold at the very thought. But he did not let his fear get the better of him, and thought ahead: once he was down on the ground, after all, he could then work out how to undo this unfair bargain. So he agreed, telling the magician that he would, most sadly, give up his sweetheart in return for being set free.

Hearing this, the magician blew upon him, and the next moment the man came back down to the ground, no longer under the power of the wind. He was overjoyed, able to walk and move freely once more rather than spinning in circles above everything. But there was the downside, something hard now he had to do.

The man hurried home as fast as he could. His betrothed cried out at the sight of him, for she had thought him lost and gone forever. She cried, but he gently walked past her, going into the house to meet her father. His own eyes were far from dry as he told the farmer that he could not work for him any longer or marry his daughter as had been intended. The farmer was amazed and confused as he heard the words and took in the sorry sight of the thin and pale man before him. He demanded to know why this must be so, and so the returned man told him everything.

Surprisingly, the farmer did not appear downhearted when he heard the whole story. He told the poor young man not to fret, before taking up a purse filled with coin and setting out. The farmer went to a witch for help, asking her advice on the situation that his future son-in-law found himself in. It was evening when the farmer returned home, smiling and in good cheer. He told the young man to go himself to the witch before dawn; if he did, then everything would be well again.

Heartened by this, the exhausted man went to bed and was soon sound asleep. Despite his weariness, he was awake well before daylight, and set off to visit the witch as instructed. She was crouched before a fire when he found her, burning herbs, and she told him to stand by and wait. Although the weather was calm, suddenly a strong wind came as if from nowhere, so powerful that it made the hut shake before them. Unperturbed, the witch led the man into her yard, before telling him to look upwards. He did as she instructed, only to see none other than the magician who had treated him so badly, whirling round and round in the air as he had done such a short while ago. The magician was in a sorry state, clad only in his nightshirt, powerless to do anything against him.

The witch assured the man that the magician would not be able to hurt him any more. Not only that, but he would suffer the same punishment that he had meted out. The witch also instructed the man on what to do if he wanted the magician to witness his wedding, an extra punishment for the way he had treated him.

The exultant young man ran home to tell his betrothed the wonderful news. A month later the two were married, the day a wonderful one to behold. While everyone was busy celebrating and dancing, the young man made his way into the yard and looked up into the sky. There, as promised, was the magician, spinning in the air above the hut, round and round and round. Taking careful aim, the man took a knife – a new one – and threw it upwards as hard as he could. The magician plummeted to the ground, but he could not move; he was nailed by the foot to the ground. There he stood, forced to watch through the window the great happiness and celebration of the wedding that he had tried so hard to ruin.

The next morning, there was no sign of the magician. According to some, they saw him flying over a large lake several miles away, surrounded by a large flock of great black crows. He was still flying, on and on, continuing his punishment.

SOMEWHERE OVER THE RAINBOW: Rainbows in Myth and Legend

There is little that can compare with the brilliance of a rainbow arching across a sunlit sky. This multicoloured optical illusion, caused by light striking water droplets in the air, often lingers for only a few moments, but this brevity only adds to their mystery, fuelling the myriad tales and beliefs in existence about this awe-inducing phenomenon.

One of the most familiar ideas from Abrahamic traditions is that the rainbow represents a covenant or promise: in Genesis in the Bible, the rainbow symbolizes God's promise never to destroy all life on earth with floodwater again. Aside from the story of the Nativity, the story of Noah and the ark is perhaps one of the most popular Bible stories taught to children from a young age, the image of the rainbow one of the earliest introductions to the Bible.

Another motif linking rainbows with the heavens is that they are a connection between the worlds of the gods and humankind. According to Norse mythology, a burning rainbow bridge spans the space between Asgard, where the gods reside, and Midgard, otherwise known as earth. The resplendent bridge known as Bifröst or Bilfrost is so huge in size that it can be seen not only from Midgard, but from all of the nine realms. This rainbow bridge is said to have a variety of meanings, including the 'blinking or winking mile', 'shimmering path', the 'fleetingly glimpsed rainbow' or 'the swaying road to heaven'.

Bifröst is guarded by the god Heimdallr or Heimdall who lives at Himinbjorg, at the Asgard end of the rainbow bridge: the perfect sentry, Heimdall needs very little sleep, is said to be able to see a distance of 100 leagues, and can hear the sound of grass growing. He is also said to possess a horn called Gjallarhorn – the yelling horn – so powerful, it can be heard in every realm. Heimdall guards Asgard against the Jötnar from the realm of Jötunheimr, an ultimately futile effort as their coming is foretold along with Ragnarok, the end of the world. The destruction of Bifröst is also foretold: Heimdall's horn will warn that Ragnarok, the terrible war to end the world, is starting, and on that day, the rainbow bridge will be no more.

It is also said of Bifröst that when a thunderstorm comes to an end and Thor leaves Asgard, the bridge grows hot from the heat of the sun. The gods travel each day over Bifröst to reach their judgement seat, situated beneath the third root of Yggdrasil, the World Tree.

In pre-Hindu Indonesian belief, the rainbow was also a connection between the gods and humankind, enabling contact between the mortal world and the gods. From the Torajan people of Indonesia, there is an image of a priestess in a trance next to a sick person, using a rainbow as a boat or a bridge to ascend to heaven to obtain spiritual strength on their behalf. Priests from the Ngaju people of Borneo drew a map of the Other World, showing a rainbow as a link between earth and heaven.

Many cultures have deities or spirits that are described as the personification or representation of the rainbow. The Greek goddess Iris is one such figure, acting as a link between the realms of god and man. Iris is portrayed in a variety of ways, the most common being as an actual rainbow, or as a young woman with splendid golden wings. Iris used rainbows to transport her as she carried messages between the gods and the mortal world, and was also known as a messenger goddess. In addition, Iris was charged with transporting water in a ewer from the River Styx, to be used when a god or goddess needed to make an oath. Woe betide the deity who dared lie; the water would leave them unconscious for the period of a year.

Another personification of the rainbow is the Mesopotamian Manzat, one of the main goddesses in Elamite culture in southwest Iran. Her name means 'rainbow' in Akkadian, and it has been suggested that she might have been a protective goddess towards women. In Hawaiian tradition there is Anuenue, another rainbow messenger goddess. She delivers messages from her brothers, the gods Kanaloa and Tane, and is able to move in the twinkling of an eye. Sometimes she is depicted as being wrapped in the colours of the rainbow, and sometimes she is the rainbow itself.

Rainbow serpent deities are common among the cultures of many Indigenous Australian groups; their names are many and differ from group to group, but they are frequently considered to be creator deities and are also often said to control the rain. There are also rainbow spirits found within several West African religions, such as the Ayida-Weddo from Haitian Vodou in Benin and Oxumere, from the Ifa religion of the Yoruba people.

As with several other bodies in the sky, it is a popular belief that you should not point at a rainbow: one researcher discovered this belief was common to 124 cultures across the globe. The consequences of breaking this taboo vary: depending on where you are, the offending finger could be bent like a rainbow, be overcome with maggots, or even fall off altogether! To the Karen people of Burma and Thailand, if a rainbow was accidentally pointed at, then a person would press their finger into their navel in order to avoid it falling off. Less specific consequences include the belief that general bad luck would befall the pointer, or someone related or significant to them. Pointing at a rainbow could also risk bringing rain back again after it had stopped.

According to a belief recorded in Shetland, Scotland, in the early 20th century, a rainbow arching over a house meant there would soon be a death either within the house or of a relation of the family who lived there. There is also the belief that 'a rainbow in the morning will give a sailor warning, a rainbow at night is the sailor's delight'.

What lies at the end of the rainbow and how to get there are questions that have taxed many. The Leprechaun – a mischievous supernatural being from Irish folklore – is said to live there with his fabled pot of gold. Although many have searched, they are doomed to failure: it is impossible to find the end of the rainbow, as it is actually a circle!

Rainbow-bridge imagery is often used today when a beloved pet or animal has passed. They are said to have crossed over the rainbow bridge to the afterlife, where they meet with other pets who have gone before, and where they will be waiting to meet their owners when their time likewise comes.

Today the rainbow is also a symbol of hope, inclusion and diversity, in particular for members and allies of the LGBTQ+ community. It was also a popular symbol of hope and unity during the recent Covid-19 pandemic.

THE LUCKY RAINBOW
AND THE INDALO MYTH

This intriguing image of a man holding a rainbow was
discovered in 1868 in the cave of Los Letreros, Almeria,
Spain. Discovered by Antonio Gongónia y Martinez,
the symbol became known as the Indalo Man, and is
believed to date back to prehistory.

One interpretation of the Indalo image is that it
shows a prehistoric god. According to this theory, the
rainbow represents a covenant of protection between
the god and mankind. Others believe that the Indalo
is actually a depiction of a hunter holding a bow
above his head.

The Indalo is linked to the revival of the Almerian
town of Mojácar in the mid-20th century, following
intellectual, artistic and financial improvements in the
area. The artistic movement there took the Indalo as their
symbol, and it was thus linked to rejuvenation and hope.

Today, the Indalo is the recognised symbol of
Almeria and Mojacar in particular. Fully embraced by
inhabitants, it is a familiar sight on the front of houses,
believed to offer protection from bad weather and the
Evil Eye, as well as being a general protective symbol.
The Indalo is also popular among tourists, depicted on
numerous souvenirs.

THE BUTTERFLY
LOVERS AND
THE COLOURS OF
THE RAINBOW

In neighbouring villages in China lived the Liang family and the Chu family. To the one was born a son known as Hsienpo, to the other, a daughter known as Yingt'ai. Young Yingt'ai was both beautiful and very clever: not content with the lot of girls of her station, she begged to be allowed to attend school. Her father finally agreed but, due to such education being denied to those of her sex, she was to go in disguise, dressed as a boy.

At school, Yingt'ai and the youth Hsienpo quickly became friends. They studied together, spent their free time together, and were nigh on inseparable, even at times sharing a bed in friendship. Hsienpo never suspected Yingt'ai's identity, and the girl took great pains to keep her secret even from her closest friend. All of this changed, however, when Yingt'ai's father died and her sister-in-law called her back from school. This came as a great blow, and Yingt'ai refused to abandon her education and Hsienpo, defying the order and remaining at school instead. For her feelings for Hsienpo had slowly but surely changed, with friendship deepening into love, even as the youth remained utterly unaware of her identity and her new feelings. She would marry no one but him, Yingt'ai decided, keeping the secret pledge safe in her heart.

With this in mind, she finally suggested the match to her sister-in-law, but the woman would not hear of it: their financial status had greatly decreased since the death of Yingt'ai's father, and a more profitable marriage was to be arranged for her. A match was accordingly arranged with the wealthy Doctor Ma from the village. Yingt'ai protested, but her words fell on deaf ears and a date was set for the marriage. In order to prevent any show of defiance, Yingt'ai's money was cut off, so she had no choice but to leave school and return home. With many tears she did so, the faithful Hsienpo going with her half of the way. In a final attempt to change her fate, Yingt'ai tried in song to tell her friend of her identity and how she felt for him, but the hapless youth did not understand her meaning, and they parted with her in tears.

Lonely and missing his friend, Hsienpo wrote to Yingt'ai frequently, but received nothing in response. Increasingly worried and missing his companion, Hsienpo visited Yingt'ai's home, asking to see his friend, Mr Yingt'ai. There was only a Miss Yingt'ai, he was told by a confused servant, due to be married soon. Due to this, she could not leave her room, and he must leave immediately, before her honour was compromised.

Too late, Hsienpo realized the bitter truth. Broken, he made his way home. There, under some of Yingt'ai's books, he discovered letters and writings declaring her love for him, and how she would marry him and no other. Poor Hsienpo, sick with grief, did not eat or drink, and fell into a terrible decline. He did not last long, dying from a broken heart.

There were no limits to Yingt'ai's grief when she learned of his passing. She cared for nothing and no one now, and resigned herself to her marriage, allowing them to place her in the bridal chair to go to her new husband. On the journey, they passed by Hsienpo's grave: she could not go by without stopping and pleaded to be allowed to pause there. Her attendants took pity on her and agreed, and at the grave poor Yingt'ai threw herself down and sobbed her heart out. She could not be induced to move for a good long while; finally her attendants helped her to her feet, but still she lingered. The despairing young woman made a silent plea: if they were truly meant to be together, then let Hsienpo open his grave three feet wide.

A sound boomed and, much to the astonishment of those looking on, the grave opened before them. Before anyone could stop her, Yingt'ai seized her chance and jumped in; the grave closed over her, leaving her attendants holding two small pieces of fabric from her dress where they had tried in vain to catch her. To their astonishment, when they let them go, they transformed into butterflies.

The jilted Doctor Ma raged when he heard what had happened, and ordered the grave to be opened. Imagine the surprise of everyone to discover not the two lovers, but instead, two white stones. In anger, those that opened the grave cast the stones onto the road, only for a bamboo, with two stems, to spring up immediately. Fearing the magic that had brought this to be, they hacked it down with a knife, but they were to be thwarted yet again: each time another shot up, again and again, until they cut them both down together. Before they could rejoice at their success, however, the cut stems again eluded them. Determined to be together, they flew into the sky to the heavens.

It is there that the pair wait until rain comes and clouds cover the sky from view, allowing them to be together as they could not be on earth. You can still see them today: for the red in the rainbow is none other than Hsienpo, the blue, Yingt'ai, together at last.

SHIMMERING LIGHTS AND WALRUS HEADS:
The Folklore and Legends of the Auroras

O ver 19,000km (12,000 miles) apart at opposite poles of the earth, fantastic displays of flashing bright lights in myriad colours and patterns swirl and dance across the sky, leaving those who witness them awestruck at their grandness and beauty. These mystical lights are known as the auroras: those at the North Pole are called the aurora borealis, or the northern lights, while aurora australis is the name by which the southern lights at the South Pole are known. They are caused when solar winds and the earth's magnetic field collide; the particles this creates in turn collide with gas atoms and the energy created is released as light. For a great deal of history, however, this was unknown, and the lights, both feared and revered, have been interpreted in many different ways by many different peoples.

The northern lights, aurora borealis, were named after the Roman goddess of the dawn and god of the north wind respectively. The aurora borealis is visible mainly from Finland, Norway, northern areas of Sweden, Iceland, southern Greenland, Alaska and Canada.

A common belief about the northern lights was that they were the souls of the dead. According to belief in some Inuit groups, when someone died their soul went to either the upper world or the under world. In a reversal of more typical associations, the under world was the better option; warm, comfortable, with food in abundance, there were none of the shortages and bitter cold those in the upper world had to suffer. Those who were lucky enough to go to the under world were known as the *arssartut* or 'ball players', as there these souls played a game of ball with the head of a walrus. The aim of the game was to kick the skull and make sure it fell with the tusks downwards, sticking in the ground; it was this impact that caused the lights in the sky. The sound the lights made was also explained by this game: the noises were made by the footsteps of the players on the frosty ground. If you wanted to have a close encounter with the lights you need only whistle: they would then come closer to investigate. Another explanation for the noises of the lights from the Inuit peoples near Hudson Bay was that they were the spirits of the dead as they tried to speak with those left on earth: if you wanted to send a message to the dead, it was said you should whisper it in return.

A spectacular display of the aurora can also be seen from the Hebrides in Scotland. There the lights were known as the Nimble Men or the Merry Dancers. Giant but graceful, these groups sometimes danced together, and at other times warred against each other, creating the lights as they moved. The heroes of the Nimble Men were split into two clans; one wore garments of white, while the other was clad in a shade of pale yellow. The females of both groups wore various colours, brightly arrayed in greens, reds, silvery white and resplendent purples.

The Inuit of the east coast of Greenland believed that the lights were the dancing souls of children born dead, premature or murdered. In some beliefs, these spirits were playing ball with their afterbirth, thus causing the lights.

Another common belief was that the lights were fires lit by groups of people. To the Anishinabe of the north-eastern United States and south-eastern Canada, in particular the Anishinaabeg, the lights were a sign from the creator of the world, Nanabozho. When he left them to head northwards to live, he reassured his people that they would always be of great importance to him: he would light fires from time to time as proof of this, and they would see the reflection of those fires in the sky.

The Kwih-dich-chuh-ahtx or the Makah Nation of Cape Flattery, Washington, believed that the lights were the fires of a small tribe that lived on the ice; the lights came from the fires they boiled whale blubber upon. The people were said to be half the height of a canoe paddle, but despite their diminutive size they were known for their great strength – it was said they could catch whales with ease with their bare hands.

Some believe that these lights are caused by foxes dashing through the snow, sparks flying from their tails as they pass. Reflecting this belief, in Finland the lights are known as *revontulet*, or 'fox fire', and the 2019 short film *Fox Fires* is a beautifully

animated retelling of the Finnish story of the origin of the mysterious lights.

Although the lights are mostly visible from coastal areas, at times the northern lights can be viewed from further inland. In areas where the lights were seen less frequently, they tended to be perceived with more negative connotations, often seen as terrible omens, foretelling death, destruction and disaster. In northern England, they were often seen as fiery spears, particularly in Northumberland. There they were also referred to as Derwentwater's lights – it was said that the lights had been bright and vibrant in the sky after the young, popular Earl of Derwentwater was executed for treason in February 1716.

Even those who were more used to the lights did not always see them positively. To the Inuit of Point Barrow, Alaska, the lights were greatly feared, and people would carry a knife for protection against them.

There are fewer tales of the southern lights, by dint of there being fewer people to observe them in those areas, but there are some intriguing similarities between the origin stories of the southern and northern lights. Some northern Australian groups believed the lights to be fires from the feasts of the Oola Pikka – ghostly spirits that spoke to male elders through the aurora. In New Zealand, it was said that Maori travellers voyaged far south in their canoes but were trapped; generations therefore remained there, and the lights were from the bonfires they lit. The lights were known as Tahu-nui-a-Rangi – 'Great Glowing of the Sky'.

FLYING CRYPTIDS

Throughout history there have been tales of strange creatures seen flying through the skies, beings that terrify us and yet at the same time intrigue us, with each fresh sighting further fuelling the desire to know more and, perhaps, even see them for ourselves. These 'cryptids' – animals or creatures whose existence is unsubstantiated or disputed – have a huge following today, peppered throughout popular culture and in some cases even being huge tourist pulls. Here are two of the most famous and well-known cryptids from the United States of America.

The Jersey Devil

The creature known as the Jersey Devil is said to frequent the New Jersey Pine Barrens in the USA. Reports of strange noises, wailings and sightings coming from the forests have been reported for decades, with those who believe they have witnessed the creature describing a two-legged beast, often kangaroo-like in appearance, sometimes with a face like a horse and a head like a collie dog. It is generally said to have two short front legs that it holds up when walking – and, of course, wings. It has also variously been described as either like a bat or a pony.

Although many are familiar with the name, it might surprise people to know that the Jersey Devil is actually one of the USA's oldest cryptids, its origins dating back to over 250 years ago. The 'devil' was not known as the Jersey Devil then however, but the Leeds Devil, named, according to some, after an association with Daniel Leeds, a 17th-century Quaker-cum-Almanac writer who got on the wrong side of the Quaker authorities and left the church under a cloud due to his mystical writings. Referred to as 'evil' on more than one occasion by contemporaries, and with the connection further fuelled by the inclusion of a winged monster on the Leeds family crest, by the close of the 18th century the Leeds Devil was firmly established in Pine Barrens folklore.

The most common explanation for the 'devil' is that it was the child of 'Mother Leeds'. With 12 children already, and expecting her 13th, some say she cursed the child, either while still pregnant or during labour, declaring 'let it be the devil'. After birth, the child was said to have turned into a terrible winged creature and flown off up the chimney, and thus the Leeds Devil was born.

In some versions, the creature stayed with the family for some years before flying off. In others, Mother Leeds looked after the creature until she died, at which point the devil flew off into the forest, where it has lived ever since. Often, Mother Leeds is said to have been a witch, the father of the child being Satan himself.

Some believe that the story stems from Daniel Leeds' son Japheth and his wife Deborah: the couple had 12 children, and some say that this was the origin of the story. According to some versions, the beast killed the whole family before it flew off.

Supposed sightings and encounters continued throughout the years. One of the stranger reports was in the 1870s, when a fisherman said that he saw the creature in the company of a mermaid. In 1893, in another encounter, a railroad engineer claimed that his train was attacked by none other than the Leeds Devil, the creature having a face like a monkey.

Some famous names also claimed to have seen the devil, one being the brother of none other than Napoleon Bonaparte. Joseph Bonaparte, former King of Spain, moved to America in exile after his forced abdication in 1813. He built a mansion at Bordentown, New Jersey, and according to the tale, when he was hunting alone in the woods near his home one day he spotted some strange tracks in the snow. Noting that one foot print was slightly larger than the other, he followed them until they came to an abrupt stop: hearing hissing, Bonaparte turned to find a large creature with a horse-like head, wings, and legs like a bird. After a tense moment where they stared at each other, the creature hissed again, before flying off.

It was not until the early 20th century that the creature's name changed from the Leeds Devil to the Jersey Devil, marking the modern era of the legend. In perhaps the most well-known sighting of the devil, in 1909, E.P. Weeden, a local councilman in Trenton, New Jersey, woke one January morning to flapping wings outside his bedroom window. When he went to investigate, cloven footprints were in the snow outside. This sparked off a spate of sightings of strange footprints and hundreds of people came forward to say they had seen the creature that made them. The Jersey Devil sightings spread to even further afield, to Delaware and Pennsylvania, until the mania finally died down.

The Jersey Devil, however, was not forgotten. In 1937, in Downingtown, Chester County, there was great excitement when Cydney Ladley, his wife, and a neighbour of the couple dashed into town one night, declaring they had seen the Jersey Devil on a back road near where they lived. According to Ladley, the creature – the size of a kangaroo, hopping, with long hair and terrible eyes – had jumped across the road in front of his car. In response, around two dozen men and a pack of dogs set off armed with guns and clubs to try and find the creature; their hunt was ultimately unsuccessful. In 1939, the Jersey Devil was given the honour of being declared the official state demon for New Jersey, further cementing the creature's fame.

There are still sightings of the devil today, with people insisting they have seen the creature. In 2015, for example, Dave Black of Little Egg Harbor captured what he claimed was photographic evidence of the devil: he witnessed it running through trees, before spreading large, leathery-looking wings and flying away over a golf course. The photo is considered unconvincing by experts. There is still a reward waiting for anyone who can capture the devil; in 1960,

Camden merchants offered $10,000 to anyone who could bring in the creature. Unsurprisingly, it has yet to be claimed.

Mothman

Although having a more recent pedigree than the Jersey Devil, Mothman has gained a firm place as one of the most popular and well-known flying cryptids in the USA.

The first sightings of the creature that came to be known as Mothman came in November 1966, when on 12 November a humanoid flying creature was reported by a group of men near Clendenin, West Virginia. Three days later, two couples were driving together through the back roads near the old TNT plant at Point Pleasant. They got more than they bargained for when they caught sight of a huge humanoid creature with large, bat-like wings. It appeared to have its wing caught in a wire, and was pulling at one wing with large hands, trying to get it free. After watching for a while, the couples drove off, but it appeared again in front of their truck, forcing them to stop; they drove on, but the creature spread its wings and flew after them – according to the witnesses, it was flying at over 160km/h (100mph).

Word of the encounter spread, sparking a spate of sightings over the next few days: interest was slow to abate, and there were said to have been over a thousand reported sightings in the next year. Mothman was also blamed for all sorts of strange occurrences in Point Pleasant; one man said that the buzzing of his television and the disappearance of his dog were caused by the creature, and strange lights in the sky, power shortages and strange sensations were also attributed to it. Many people said they experienced a strange feeling of dread after witnessing Mothman, leading to belief that the creature was a bad omen.

Early reports of Mothman described a winged, humanoid creature with red eyes. Between 1.8 and 2m (6–7ft) tall, with large wings like a bat, it was also said to have long legs, which stretched out behind when it was flying. Other sightings described a creature that was similar to an owl in size. Intriguingly, some witnesses reported that, after seeing the creature, they were visited by strange 'men in black' at their homes. With a dull, robotic tone, these strangers probed witnesses for details, before warning them not to reveal their sighting to anyone else. Phone calls from the same robotic voice were also reported.

The last of this particular spate of sightings of Mothman came in December 1967, after the collapse of the Silver Bridge, a tragedy that led to the deaths of 46 people. Due to this supposed correlation, the two became linked in the minds of many, leading to the theory that Mothman had appeared to either predict or even cause the disaster. Not everyone believes that Mothman's presence was a negative one: there are those who say that he actually came to warn people of the tragedy.

Fresh interest in Mothman was sparked in 1975 with the release of John Keel's book, *The Mothman Prophecies*. Interest surged again in 2002 with the film of the same name starring Richard Gere, and sightings continue of this elusive being. In 2017, there were over 20 reports of a similar creature being sighted between April and July in Chicago.

The origins of the name are unclear, but are generally attributed to a reporter who was inspired by the Killer Moth character from the popular *Batman* comics at the time.

Explanations for Mothman encounters vary. With the initial sightings, the Sheriff of Mason County put forward the theory that people were actually seeing a 'shitepoke', a name given to a type of heron that was much larger than average. Another explanation is that people were actually seeing a sandhill crane which had been blown off course on migration – this giant bird, with a wingspan of around 2m (7ft), would have been an unfamiliar sight, causing

confusion and fear in those who unwittingly witnessed it. The crane stands almost as tall as a man and is the second largest crane in America. This theory is backed up by the fact that in 1966 two witnesses said that the creature they had seen was definitely a giant bird.

It is undeniable that Mothman is firmly entrenched in the psyche and folklore of Point Pleasant. This is reflected in the 3.7m (12ft) metallic Mothman statute commemorating the legend in Gunn Park, Point Pleasant. Then there is the annual Mothman Festival, which takes place on the third weekend in September and attracts thousands of visitors each year.

People don't have to wait until September, however, to get a Mothman fix. The Mothman Museum in Point Pleasant is an invaluable source of information for anyone interested in learning about Mothman, containing a wide range of documents, images and artefacts relating to the enduring legend.

Conclusion

It has only been possible to touch upon a mere fraction of the folklore and legends related to the stars and skies throughout these pages, as we have embarked together upon a magical and wondrous tour through some of the most fascinating and representative folklore from many of the world's nations and cultures.

Although we leave each other here, it is not the end: for we remain united through these humbly written words and, by extension, by the tales, superstitions and beliefs that we share and remember along with the rest of humankind. As we stated in the introduction to this volume, it is, as ever, folklore that binds us together, far more than it divides us, if only – as ever – we choose to listen.

I hope you have enjoyed the journey: remember, keep on looking upwards. You never know what you might see.

Acknowledgements

It would be impossible to thank every last person who has been involved in some way from the book's inception to finally being in print, but here are a few thank yous where space allows.

Firstly, a huge thank you to Dee Dee Chainey; without her and the fantastical journey we have been on together these last few years through #FolkloreThursday and writing the *Treasury of Folklore* books, this volume would not now be in your hands. It has been a different experience writing this one alone, but Dee Dee has never ceased to provide encouragement, opinions and her wonderful expertise throughout the entire process: thank you!

Hearty thanks are also due to the wonderful #FolkloreThursday community; although things have changed greatly over this last year, one thing remains constant: the support, camaraderie and bond that the unceasing love of all things folklore brings.

There is no denying that this has been a tough year in many ways, and I would not have got through it, much less got this book finished in time, if not for some truly wonderful friends. Too numerous to list, you know who you are: thank you!

A massive thank you to my wonderful children: Elizabeth, Alfred and Jolyon, you make every day worth it, and humour your mother when she goes hunting for her own books in Waterstones.

Finally, but by no means least, a huge thank you to everyone at Batsford for making this book a reality, and to the Sprung Sultan team for continued support throughout.

References

PART ONE: THE STARS AND HEAVENS

The Sun, Moon and Stars

First People of America and Canada, 'The Sun, Moon and Stars: A Navajo Legend', https://www.firstpeople.us/FP-Html-Legends/TheSunMoonandStars-Navajo.html (accessed 16/6/2022)

Solar Deities: Gods and Goddesses of the Sun

AMATERASU

Kazuo, Matsumura, '"Alone among Women": A Comparative Mythic Analysis of the Development of Amaterasu Theology', https://www2.kokugakuin.ac.jp/ijcc/wp/cpjr/kami/matsumura.html (accessed 20/5/2022)

Yoshida, Atsuhiko, 'Association of the Sun and the Rice in Japanese Myths and Rituals', https://core.ac.uk/download/pdf/292912345.pdf (accessed 14/10/2022)

SAULE

Beresnevičius, Gintaras, trans. Tamošiūnienė, Lora, 'Lithuanian Religion and Mythology', https://web.archive.org/web/20140512213250/http://ausis.gf.vu.lt/eka/mythology/relmyth.html (accessed 11/6/2022)

Chase, George Davis, 'Sun Myths in Lithuanian Folksongs', *Transactions and Proceedings of the American Philological Association*, vol. 31, 1900, pp. 189–201

Enthoven, R.E., 'The Latvians in Their Folk Songs', *Folklore*, vol. 48, no. 2, 1937, pp. 183–6

UTU-SHAMASH

Beckman, Gary (2012), 'Shamash among the Hittites', in Egmond, Wolfert S. van and Soldt, Wilfred H. van (eds.), *Theory and practice of knowledge transfer: studies in school education in the ancient Near East and beyond*, Leiden: Nederlands Instituut voor het Nabije Oosten (NINO), https://www.academia.edu/48247802/Shamash_among_the_Hittites (accessed 14/9/2022)

Black, Jeremy, and Green, Anthony, *Gods, Demons and Symbols of Ancient Mesopotamia: An Illustrated Dictionary*, The British Museum Press, 1992

SÓL

Bellows, Henry Adams, *The Poetic Edda*, New York, The American-Scandinavian Foundation, 1923

Brodeur, Arthur Gilchrist (trans.), *The Prose Edda of Snorri Sturlson*, New York, The American-Scandinavian Foundation, 1916

Lindow, John, *Norse Mythology: A Guide to the Gods, Heroes, Rituals, and Beliefs*, Oxford University Press, 2001

Huītzilōpōchtli

Bancroft-Hunt, Norman, *Gods and Myths of the Aztecs*, New York, Smithmark, 1996

Phillips, Charles, *The Mythology of the Aztec & Maya*, London, Southwater, 2006

A Fateful Flight: Daedalus and Icarus

Garth, Sir Samuel and Dryden, John et al (trans.), Ovid, *Metamorphoses*, http://classics.mit.edu/Ovid/metam.8.eighth.html, (accessed 3/5/2022)

Sun-Got-Bit-By-Bear: Eclipses of the Sun

Deutsch, James, 'What Folklore Tells Us About Eclipses', https://www.smithsonianmag.com/smithsonian-institution/what-folklore-tells-us-about-eclipses-180964488/ (accessed 13/10/2022)

Knappert, Jan, *Indian Mythology: an Encyclopedia of Myth and Legend*, Hammersmith, London, The Antiquarian Press, 1991

Littmann, Mark; Espenak, Fred; and Wilcox, Ken, *Totality: Eclipses of the Sun*, Oxford, Oxford University Press, 2008

Scheub, Harold, *A Dictionary of African Mythology: the mythmaker as storyteller*, Oxford, Oxford University Press, 2000, pp. 74, 168

Why the Sun and the Moon Live in the Sky

Elphinstone, Dayrell, *Folk Stories from Southern Nigeria, West Africa*, London, Longmans, Green and Co, 1910, pp. 64–5

Hina: The Woman in the Moon

Westervelt, W.D., *Legends of Maui, A Demi-God of Polynesia*, https://www.sacred-texts.com/pac/maui/maui18.htm (accessed 15/9/2022)

Man, Rabbit, or Jack and Jill? The Many Faces of the Moon

The Man in the Moon

Baring-Gould, Sabine, *Curious Myths of the Middle Ages*, London, Rivingtons, 1876

Skeat, Walter W., *Malay Magic, being an introduction to the folklore and popular religion of the Malay Peninsula*, London, Macmillan, 1900

Thuillard, Marc, 'Analysis of the Worldwide Distribution of the "Man or Animal in the Moon" Motifs', https://www.folklore.ee/folklore/vol84/thuillard.pdf, (accessed 27/3/2022)

The Fox

Barlow, Genevieve, *Latin American Tales: From the Pampas to the Pyramids of Mexico*, USA, Rand McNally and Company, pp. 62–7

The Water Carriers

Holmberg, Uno, *Finno-Ugric Mythology; Siberian Mythology*, Boston, 1927, p. 423

The Toad

Boas, Franz (ed.), *Folktales of Salishan and Sahaptin Tribes*, New York, American Folklore Society, 1917, p. 123

Krappe, Alexander H., 'The Lunar Frog', *Folklore*, vol. 51, no. 3, 1940, pp. 161–71

Lai, Whalen, 'Recent PRC Scholarship on Chinese Myths', *Asian Folklore Studies*, vol. 53, no. 1, 1994, pp. 151–61

The Hare
Bleek, W.H., *Reynard the Fox in South Africa*, London, Trübner and Co., 1864, p. 72

Harley, Timothy, *Moon Lore,* 1885, https://www.sacred-texts.com/astro/ml/ml08.htm#fr_83 (accessed 22/9/2022) p. 62

Warren, Henry Clarke, *Buddhism in Translations, The Hare Mark in the Moon*, https://www.sacred-texts.com/bud/bits/bits056.htm (accessed 2/9/2022)

The Morning Star and the Evening Star: A Romanian Tale
Kremnitz, Mite (collected), Percival, J.M. (arranged), *Romanian Fairy Tales*, New York, H. Holt and company, 1885, pp. 121–9

The Seven Sisters: Orion and the Pleiades
'African Ethnoastronomy', Astronomical Society of Southern Africa, https://assa.saao.ac.za/astronomy-in-south-africa/ethnoastronomy/ (accessed 13/10/2022)

Avilin, Tsimafei, 'The Pleiades in the Belarusian Tradition: Folklore Texts and Linguistic Areal Studies', https://www.folklore.ee/folklore/vol72/avilin.pdf (accessed 13/10/2022)

Monroe, Jean Guard, and Williamson, R.A., *They Dance in the Sky: Native American Star Myths*, Boston, Houghton Mifflin Company, 1987

Norris, Ray P., and Norris, Barnaby R.M., 'Why Are there Seven Sisters?', https://arxiv.org/abs/2101.09170 (accessed 15/7/2022)

How the Milky Way Came to Be
Leslau, Charlotte, *African Folk Tales*, Mount Vernon, N.Y., Peter Pauper Press, 1963, p. 56

Soaring Souls and Shooting Stars: Star Superstitions from Around the World

Shooting Stars
Avilin, Tsimafei, 'Meteor Beliefs Project: East European meteor folk-beliefs', *WGN,* Journal of the IMO, 35:5 (2007), p. 113

Gheorghe, A.D., and McBeath, A., 'Romanian Meteor Mythology', *Proceedings of the International Meteor Conference, Petnica, Yugoslavia, 25–28 September 1997*, IMO, pp. 82–8

Hamacher, Duane W., and Norris, Ray P., 'Meteors in Australian Aboriginal Dreamings', *WGN,* Journal of the IMO, 38:10 (2010), p. 91

Opie, Iona, *A Dictionary of Superstitions*, Oxford University Press, 1989, p. 376

Pliny, *Natural History*, book 28, p. 37, https://archive.org/details/

naturalhistory08plinuoft/page/n13/ mode/2up?view=theater (accessed 16/7/2022)

Thomas, Daniel L. and Lucy B., *Kentucky Superstitions*, Princeton University Press, Princeton, 1920, p. 57, https://ia902700.us.archive.org/35/ items/kentuckysupersti00thomuoft/ kentuckysupersti00thomuoft.pdf (accessed 23/8/2022)

WISHING ON A STAR

Avilin, Tsimafei, 'Meteor Beliefs Project: Belarusian meteor folk-beliefs', *WGN*, Journal of the IMO, 34:4 (2006), p. 120

De Lys, Claudia, *What's So Lucky about a Four-Leaf Clover?*, Bell Publishing Company, New York, 1989, p. 421

Warren Beckwith, Martha, 'Signs and Superstitions Collected from American College Girls', *The Journal of American Folklore*, vol. 36, no. 139 (Jan–Mar 1923), pp. 113–14

POINTING AT STARS

Avilin, Tsimafei, 'Meteor Beliefs Project: East European meteor folk-beliefs', *WGN*, Journal of the IMO, 35:5 (2007), p. 114

Bainton, Roy, *The Mammoth Book of Superstition,* Robinson, 2016, p. 88

Thomas, Daniel L. and Lucy B., *Kentucky Superstitions*, Princeton University Press, Princeton, 1920, pp. 17, 46, https://ia902700. us.archive.org/35/items/ kentuckysupersti00thomuoft/ kentuckysupersti00thomuoft.pdf (accessed 23/8/2022)

WEATHER AND HARVESTS

Avilin, Tsimafei, 'Meteor Beliefs Project: Belarusian meteor folk-beliefs', *WGN*, Journal of the IMO, 34:4 (2006), pp. 119–23

Mihanovich, Clement S., 'Fortune-Telling and Superstitions among the Peasants of the Poljica Region of Dalmatia', *The Journal of American Folklore*, vol. 64, no. 252, 1951, pp. 197–202

PASSING SOULS

Avilin, Tsimafei, 'Meteor Beliefs Project: East European meteor folk-beliefs', *WGN*, Journal of the IMO, 35:5 (2007), p. 113–16

Gheorghe, A.D. and McBeath, A., 'Romanian Meteor Mythology', *Proceedings of the International Meteor Conference, Petnica, Yugoslavia, 25–28 September 1997*, IMO, pp. 82–8

McBeath, Alastair, and Gheorghe, Andrei Dorian, 'Meteor Beliefs Project: Classical beliefs connecting meteors with life and death', *WGN*, Journal of the IMO, 34:5 (2006), pp. 148–50

DRAGONS IN THE SKY

Avilin, Tsimafei, 'Meteor Beliefs Project: East European meteor folk-beliefs', *WGN*, Journal of the IMO, 35:5 (2007), pp. 113–16

Gheorghe, A.D. & McBeath, A., 'Romanian Meteor Mythology', *Proceedings of the International Meteor Conference, Petnica, Yugoslavia, 25–28 September 1997*, IMO, pp. 82–8

PART TWO: SUMPTUOUS SKIES

Stallions of the Skies: Pegasus and Other Soaring Steeds

Hesiod, *Theogony*, https://www.perseus.tufts.edu/hopper/text?doc=Perseus:text:1999.01.0130:card=270&highlight=thunder%2Cpegasus (accessed 9/7/2022)

Levin, Theodore Craig, *Where Rivers and Mountains Sing: Sound, Music and Nomadism in Tuva and Beyond*, Indiana University Press, 2006

Mani, Vettam, *Puranic Encyclopaedia: a comprehensive dictionary with special reference to the epic and Puranic literature*, Motilal Banarsidass, 1975, p. 32

Qazaqstan Tarihy, 'National Emblem of Kazakhstan', https://e-history.kz/en/news/show/7061 (accessed 20/8/2022)

Radhakrishnan, S., '10.27', *The Bhagavadgita*, Blackie & Son (India) Ltd, 1977, p. 264, https://www.sacred-texts.com/hin/vp/vp057.htm (accessed 23/7/2022)

Wilson, Horace Hayman (trans.), *Vishnu Purana: Book 1: Chapter XXII*, https://www.sacred-texts.com/hin/vp/vp044.htm#fr_236 (accessed 10/10/2022)

The Flying Wax Horse

Parker, Henry, *Village Folk-tales of Ceylon*, volume III, London, Luzac & Co, 1914, pp. 183–8

Birds of Myth and Legend

CALADRIUS

Druce, George C., 'The Caladrius and its Legend', https://bestiary.ca/etexts/druce-caladrius-and-its-legend.pdf (accessed 21/8/2022)

HUGINN AND MUNINN

Bellows, Henry Adams (trans.), *The Poetic Edda*, New York, The American-Scandinavian Foundation, 1923

Lindow, John, *Norse Mythology: A Guide to Gods, Heroes, Rituals, and Beliefs*, Oxford, Oxford University Press, 2002

ZIZ

Wazana, Nili, 'Anzu and Ziz: Great Mythical Birds in Ancient Near Eastern, Biblical and Rabbinic Traditions', *JANES* 31, 2009, pp. 111–35

FIREBIRD

Afanasyev, Alexander, and Magnus, Leonard A. (ed.), *Russian Folk Tales*, London, K. Paul, 1916

Ransome, Arthur, *Old Peter's Russian Tales*, London, New York, Thomas Nelson and sons, 1916

FENGHUANG

Zhu, Lyujie, 'Fenghuang and Phoenix: Translation of Culture', 2020, http://www.ijlll.org/vol6/263-IL006.pdf (accessed 5/5/2022)

The Firebird

Massie, Suzanne, *Land of the Firebird: The Beauty of Old Russia*, Simon and Schuster, 1980, pp. 17–18

Come Rain or Shine: Weather Lore and Superstitions

Alcock, P.G., *Rainbows in the Mist: Indigenous Weather Knowledge, Beliefs and Folklore in South Africa*, https://tww.id.au/weather/southafrica.html, (accessed 5/9/2022)

Hazen, H.A., 'The Origin and Value of Weather Lore', *The Journal of American Folklore*, vol. 13, no. 50 (Jul–Sep 1900), pp. 191–8

Swainson, C.A., *A Handbook of Weather Folk-lore*, W. Blackwood and Sons, 1873

Theophrastus, *De Signis*, http://penelope.uchicago.edu/Thayer/E/Roman/Texts/Theophrastus/De_signis*.html (accessed 12/5/2022)

Christening the Apples: Weather Forecasting with St Swithin

Ælfric of Eynsham, 'Of Saint Swythun', *Ælfric's Lives of Saints*, London, N. Trübner & Co., 1881

Met Office: Official Blog, 'Any truth in St Swithin's weather folklore?', https://blog.metoffice.gov.uk/2011/07/14/any-truth-in-st-swithin%E2%80%99s-weather-folklore/ (accessed 13/10/2022)

Raising up a Storm: Witches, Tempestarii and Weather Magic

Agobard of Lyons, *On Hail and Thunder*, Internet Medieval Source Book, https://sourcebooks.fordham.edu/source/Agobard-OnHailandThunder.asp (accessed 14/5/2022)

Bailey Michael D., *Magic and Superstition in Europe. A Concise History from Antiquity to the Present*, Rowman & Littlefield, p. 20

Dalyell, Sir John Graham, *The Darker Superstitions of Scotland*, Glasgow, R. Griffin & Co., 1835

Grimm, Jacob, *Teutonic Mythology*, London, W. Swan Sonnenschein & Allen, 1880

Mackay, Christopher S. (trans.), *The Hammer of Witches: A Complete Translation of the Malleus Maleficarum*, Cambridge University Press, 2009

Mallet, Paul Henri, *Northern Antiquities: Or, A Description of the Manners, Customs, Religion and Laws of the Ancient Danes*, Edinburgh, C. Stewart, 1809

Thomas, Keith, *Religion and the Decline of Magic*, London, Penguin Books, 1991, p. 37

Winsham, Willow, *Accused: British Witches Throughout History*, Barnsley, Pen and Sword Books, 2015

The Westray Storm Witch

'Witchcraft in the Orkney Isles', https://www.orkneyjar.com/folklore/witchcraft/stormwitch.htm (accessed 23/7/2022)

Carried Away by the Wind

Naaké, John Philophilus, *Slavonic Fairy Tales*, London, Henry S. King and Co., 1874, pp. 1–5

Somewhere Over the Rainbow: Rainbows in Myth and Legend

Bellows, Henry Adams, *The Poetic Edda*, New York, The American-Scandinavian Foundation, 1923

Blust, Robert, *Pointing, Rainbows, and the Archaeology of Mind*, Anthropos, 2021. 116. 145-162. 10.5771/0257-9774-2021-1-145.

Brodeur, Arthur Gilchrist (trans.), *The Prose Edda of Snorri Sturlson*, New York, The American-Scandinavian Foundation, 1916

Liddell, Henry George, *A Greek–English Lexicon*, New York, Harper & Brothers, 1876

Lindow, John, *Norse Mythology: A Guide to the Gods, Heroes, Rituals, and Beliefs*, Oxford University Press, 2001

Seton-Williams, M.V., *Greek Legends and Stories*, Rubicon Press, 2000, pp. 75–76

The Lucky Rainbow and the Indalo Myth

'Almeria Province – Indalo Man', https://www.andalucia.com/province/almeria/indalo/home.htm (accessed 10/10/2022)

The Butterfly Lovers and the Colours of the Rainbow

Eberhard, Wolfram, *Folktales of China*, Chicago, University of Chicago Press, 1965, p. 20–4

Shimmering Lights and Walrus Heads: The Folklore and Legends of the Auroras

Briggs, J. Morton, 'Aurora and Enlightenment Eighteenth-Century Explanations of the Aurora Borealis', *Isis*, vol. 58, no. 4, 1967, pp. 491–503

Hamacher, Duane W, *Aurorae in Australian Aboriginal Traditions*, https://web.archive.org/web/20131020181951/http://www.narit.or.th/en/files/2013JAHHvol16/2013JAHH...16..207H.pdf (Accessed: 28/3/2023)

Holzworth, Robert H. II, 'Folklore of the Aurora', https://earthweb.ess.washington.edu/bobholz/Holzworth_folklore_EO056i010p00686_rga.pdf (accessed 5/7/2022)

Nansen, Fridtjof, *Eskimo Life*, London, Longmans, Green, and Co., 1894, p. 235

Rink, H., *Tales and Traditions of the Eskimo*, Edinburgh, London, W. Blackwood and Sons, 1875, p. 37

Savage, Candace Sherk, *Aurora: The Mysterious Northern Lights*, San Francisco, Sierra Club Books, 1994

Swan, James Gilchrist, *The Indians of Cape Flattery*, Washington, Smithsonian Institution, 1870, p. 87

Weyer, E.M., *The Eskimos, Their Environment and Folkways*, Hamden, Connecticut, Archon, 1969, p. 243

Flying Cryptids

The Jersey Devil

McCrann, Grace-Ellen, 'Legend of the New Jersey Devil', The New Jersey Historical Society, 26 October 2000, https://web.archive.org/web/20140902163244/http://www.jerseyhistory.org/legend_jerseydevil.html (accessed 22/11/2022)

Regal, Brian, 'The Jersey Devil: The Real Story', *Skeptical Inquirer*, vol. 37, no. 6, November/December 2013, https://skepticalinquirer.org/2013/11/the-jersey-devil-the-real-story/ (accessed 12/6/2022)

Schlosser, S.E., 'Joseph Bonaparte and the Jersey Devil', American Folklore, https://web.archive.org/web/20100202013405/http://www.americanfolklore.net/folktales/nj6.html (accessed 5/7/2022)

Mothman

Mart, T.S., *A Guide to Sky Monsters: Thunderbirds, the Jersey Devil, Mothman, and Other Flying Cryptids*,

Indiana, Red Lightning Books, 2021 'Couples See Man-Sized Bird ... Creature ... Something', *Point Pleasant Register*, Point Pleasant, WV, 16 November 1966, https://web.archive.org/web/20071011230219/http://www.westva.net/mothman/1966-11-16.htm (accessed 12/11/2022)

'Monster Bird with Red Eyes May Be Crane', *The Gettysburg Times*, 1 December 1966, https://news.google.com/newspapers?id=LG-0mAAAAIBAJ&pg=620,2790721&d-q=point+pleasant+roger+scarber-ry&hl=en (accessed 22/11/2022)

'Eight People Say They Saw "Creature"', *Williamson Daily News*, 18 November 1966, https://news.google.com/newspapers?id=XyNEAAAAIBAJ&pg=959,3488207 (accessed 15/11/2022)

Index